Indiscretions

Barbara Winkes

ISBN: 978-1-0690835-5-5

Cover art © May Dawney Designs

Created with Atticus

For D.

Chapter One

I t took her twenty minutes to walk home from the bar, fifteen on a good day. Run by a retired cop and near the precinct, the *Code 7* was a popular hangout for Ellie and her colleagues. The night was chillier than she'd expected, the thin cardigan hardly enough to ward off the wind. As she walked along the street, her heels clicked on the concrete. Ellie kept her head up high, her gaze straight ahead, even when there where whistles and catcalls from the car passing her by.

She might have run their license plate the next day to see if she could turn up any unpaid tickets, but tonight, she had too many other things on her mind. Leaving the strip of bars and restaurants behind, she crossed the street to enter a more residential-looking neighborhood. Rent was one of the issues to worry about. Her roommate had moved out without much of a notice, leaving her a check to cover her part for one month. Ellie would be able to make do for a while, but she didn't want to pay that much money for a whole lot of empty space.

She wasn't worried about the upcoming evaluation. Her performance reviews had never been anything but excellent. She knew how to do the job, had the skills and the intuition, and the ambition to go further. Ellie liked to hang out with her colleagues after work, but there was no doubt about who held the most coveted positions. They were rock stars. She wanted to be one of them, as soon as possible.

At the next corner, a man she guessed to be in his twenties came jogging around the hedge, wearing a hoodie, music blasting from his earbuds. They came close to colliding, and she nearly stumbled on the high heels she preferred to wear after work.

"I'm sorry, Ma'am. I didn't see you."

He held up his hands to demonstrate he meant no harm. She shrugged and walked on, thinking that between him possibly being almost deaf and her not paying attention, they'd been equally guilty.

Another broken streetlight. She sighed in exasperation. So far, all the city had gotten from the new mayor was a lot of promises and budget cuts. This wasn't safe. She made a mental note to harass somebody about it the next day.

Ten minutes away from home. She longed for a hot bath and eight solid hours of sleep before her next shift. Oblivion. She didn't want to waste another thought on the evaluation, having to move anytime soon, or the fact that her hair color was from a bottle because Rhonda had said she preferred blondes. She shouldn't be thinking about the detective she knew to be in a relationship, who had given her the eye across the bar, either. Maybe it had been Ellie's imagination, because she'd been frustrated, and lonely, and had too much to drink.

The gloved hand clamping around her throat came out of nowhere, jolting her out of her mildly unpleasant musings into a disturbing reality. She kicked with her feet, reaching up to claw at his eyes instead of trying to remove the hand. The iron grip eased up enough for her to take a breath. A well-placed blow with her elbow, and he let her go, but shoved her hard enough to make her fall flat on her face. He was strong. The attacker had obviously waited for her. He grabbed her ankle and dragged her towards the gate of the nearest house, her knees painfully scraping over the concrete. Still, she struggled to get out of his grip, stumbling to her feet. The man was wearing a ski mask, his eyes glinting menacingly in the dark as he advanced on her once more, wrestling her to the ground. Ellie was sure she was going to pass out when the back of her head connected with the sidewalk, but she remained much aware of the blinding pain. He slapped her, hard. She wriggled under him, trying to bend her legs enough so she could kick him where it hurt. Those heels had to be good for something, damn it. Go for the eyes again. He held down her wrists, slamming down her hands until she was sure some bones had to be broken. Pain. Chill.

"Stop...struggling!" he hissed.

Cold sweat. She smelled like fear. Why did all the windows stay dark? Somebody had to notice what was going on, somebody...They both froze at the sound of police sirens, close, no more than a couple of streets away. The pressure eased up, but a moment later, she cried out from the sharp, burning pain in her shoulder. The man disappeared into the night. As the squad car sped around the corner, Ellie closed her eyes.

Ellie Harding was aware of the looks following her when she walked into the station that morning. She had fervently wished for this moment and dreaded it at the same time. She wanted to move on with her life and had told the department psychiatrist so. Over time, her assurances had become more credible, apparently, because she had been cleared for active duty. Kate, Libby, Jensen, and Chris came over to greet her at the door for affectionate pats on the shoulder. Her stance had to signal clearly, no hugs. Even Sergeant Bristol joined them. Ellie thanked each of them with a polite smile, waiting for the niceties to be over.

No more desk duty, no more visits to the psychiatrist in the near future. She could finally breathe again—at least she'd thought so. Time would tell, but this was infinitely better than staring at the walls in her home and fielding off concerned phone calls or offers to come visit from her friends and Rhonda.

Frankly, Ellie didn't think she'd handled herself the way she should have during the attack. She wanted to do the best she could to forget about it altogether, at least the part where it happened to her. Her assailant hadn't been caught yet, which made it impossible to completely ban him from her mind, and everyone else's. He was still out there. He might try the same shit with other women or had done it before. Ellie wished she'd had a chance to rip the mask off his ugly face. She forced her attention back to the chatter among her colleagues as they headed for roll call.

Ellie sat with Jensen, starting a bit when her gaze fell on the woman standing next to the sergeant. They were talking in hushed tones. She looked tired, but there was grim determination in her expression. Ellie remembered the flirtatious smile she had sent in her direction that night at the bar, what seemed like forever ago.

Detective Jordan Carpenter, Homicide, one of the rock stars. Bristol would possibly assign one or more officers to work with her today. Ellie prayed they'd pick her. After her unplanned detour from her spotless career, she needed something of a boost. For said career, and maybe, for her ego too.

"There's been a breakthrough. This morning, one of the victims was found alive. We are now tracing her last steps before the abduction, and any connections to the other victims. Lori Gleason was reported missing by a friend she was supposed to meet, last seen in a coffee shop in the city center around 10.00 a.m. on June sixth. She remembers the coffee shop, but nothing after that."

Despite the warm pleasant timbre to her voice, Ellie could sense the detective's frustration underneath. Everyone knew the case she was referring to. The first murder victim had been found in the basement of an empty office building, the second one behind a dumpster. The results of each autopsy had connected the two, specific ligature marks, fibers from the same rope, the same choice of torture. Ellie shuddered. She had to remind herself she was here, alive, and what had happened to her was nothing like what these women had endured. She could make a difference. Eventually, they would stop him from ever hurting another woman—the killer as well as the man who had jumped her on her way home.

"Robbins and McCarthy, you'll be with Detective Carpenter," Sergeant Bristol said. Carpenter nodded. "Those abductions happened within a radius of less than seven miles," she added. "Seems like our guy is not moving much, but he has been escalating. The first victim was found last fall, the other two within a couple of months. He's bound to make mistakes."

Ellie couldn't believe what she'd heard. They couldn't overlook her. Not today. She raised her hand, pleased to see a hint of recognition on Carpenter's face.

"The victim you found alive, where was she?" Ellie asked.

"In the basement of a move-in ready suburban home," Jordan said. "The owners just closed last week. You get any calls regarding empty buildings, for sale, refer straight to us—and be careful. This is one sadistic son of a bitch." That was directed at everyone in the room. Ellie felt dismissed, but she wasn't willing to take it. As her colleagues filed out of the room, Libby was waiting for her, but instead of joining her, Ellie hurried to meet up with Sergeant Bristol and the detective.

"I was cleared for active duty," she said.

"I am aware of that, Officer Harding."

"Why am I not working with the detectives today? Is there something in my evaluation that suggests..."

"No, there isn't."

Ellie was aware of the curious glance the detective cast her way before she went back to studying her file. "You know I was planning to take the exam next year. I could use the experience."

"You'll have the chance to get it, just not today." His tone was final. "In case you have forgotten, it's your *first* day back on active duty. Your assignment is not a punishment."

"Sir," she said tersely and turned to walk away.

"Are you okay?" Libby asked.

Ellie wasn't okay. She wasn't sure she'd ever be, but she had to keep doing her job. Otherwise, she'd go insane sometime soon. "Let's go."

The day was successful enough, with the two of them arresting a dealer trying to recruit high school kids, answering a domestic disturbance call that deescalated quickly before anyone could get killed. The urge to kill—Ellie could understand it when she got a glimpse at the couple's desolate life, and she was happy to let Libby make that arrest. She was painfully aware of how close her own emotions hovered under the surface, memories of helplessness and fading bruises that made her want to harm the man. Accompanying the woman to the shelter wasn't much better, she realized later. Reminders, everywhere, every day. She had to stop it, or she wouldn't be able to do her job.

Ellie hated the relief that came with taking off her uniform that night. She couldn't let him do that to her.

"Are you coming with us?" Libby asked. Ellie thought this might be a good opportunity for free drinks, but she declined. She hadn't gone back to the *Code 7* since the attack, as if the venue was somehow responsible, and she wasn't planning on going tonight. A beer at home would do. Libby didn't try hard to convince her, exposing her conflict. They wanted to welcome her back, but the way her peers seemed to struggle with how to act around her, was making her crazy. It was as if she had taught them something no one wanted to know—they were vulnerable too. They might be confronted with that fact every now and then, but one of their own barely escaping with their own life... you couldn't spell it out any clearer. Ellie hoped they'd come to their senses sometime soon because she wasn't going anywhere.

"Officer Harding."

She spun around to see Detective Carpenter had walked up behind her, ready to leave as well.

"Detective," she mumbled, not in the mood for small talk after today's disappointment.

"How was your first day back?"

Ellie was pretty sure making conversation wasn't the plan here. She was conflicted. Part of her wanted to make sure both Carpenter and Bristol knew she didn't consider their decision as fair. Another part remembered how Jordan had shown interest back then, at the bar. Ellie needed something flattering, something to tell her life would go on, but the question was, should she take it from someone who was in a committed relationship, more or less? Ellie didn't know if it was more or less, but she had heard talk about the detective.

She shrugged. "Same old. I'd been hoping for something different to brush up my résumé, but obviously, it didn't happen."

"I've taken a look at your résumé," Jordan said as they walked along the hallway. "It looks fine to me. You aced every single test and evaluation."

"Exactly," Ellie snapped, but stopped herself before she might say anything she would regret later. With Jordan Carpenter, it was wise to tread carefully. Ellie wanted to work in her squad one day. Pissing her off was not the best start.

"I'm sorry. It's no one's fault. I had hoped everyone would treat me the same way as before once I was off desk duty. A guy beat me up on a dark street. That's embarrassing. It's not contagious."

"It's neither. I don't think anyone's treating you differently. Choosing the officers today was not a matter of preference."

"Was the woman able to tell you anything?"

Her lips formed a thin line. "She's in shock, lost track of time. She says she never saw his face. He wore a mask the whole time. So, we have nothing on that front."

Ellie had more questions, but against her will, she was drawn back into her own memories, the time at the hospital, the tests, staff speaking to her in soft tones, regarding her with sympathetic looks. She had hated every moment of it. She had hated being stuck behind a desk, waiting to be cleared for active duty.

"We are still piecing the details together," Jordan told her. "We might need some more help. I'll ask for you."

"Really?" For a moment, excitement won over all conflicted feelings she might harbor towards the woman.

Jordan laughed. "I hope you won't be too disappointed. The way I see it, if you're up to going out on the streets, you're definitely up to making calls and wading through tons of paper. We'll find you something to do."

"Thank you. You're not going out with the others tonight?"

"Oh no. I'll go home for a few hours and try to get some sleep. You should too. I'll expect you bright and early."

"Maybe...you'd like to come have a beer at my place, just one, to wind down?" Ellie was testing the waters. They had arrived at her car.

Jordan gave her a long look, apparently not opposed to the offer or anything it implied.

"Another time, I'd love to. Good night, Ellie." She gave her the sympathetic pat on the shoulder Ellie had gotten from everyone else today and smiled, promise or pretense, it was hard to tell.

"Sure. No problem. See you tomorrow."

Ellie watched her walk away, taking notice of the sway of her hips. "Another time, I'd love to," she muttered under her breath, imitating her. "Do you prefer blondes too?"

⁂

Ellie hadn't told the psychiatrist the whole truth, fearing he might reconsider his decision. She wasn't a danger to herself or anyone else, and she'd proven it today. If she hadn't been able to make a good judgment call, she might have shot the abuser in the knee—or elsewhere—instead of handing him over to Libby. She might have yelled at the woman who had, halfway on the way to the shelter, wondered if everything was her fault. Ellie had a fairly good grip on her emotions and perceptions, but she had neglected to share with the psychiatrist the vow she'd made.

From now on, she'd take from life whatever she wanted. She had spent so much time trying to please others, family, teachers, superiors, always thinking there would come a moment when she'd put herself first. She could have been killed, or raped, because of one asshole making that decision.

Life *owed* her. Ellie was going to collect.

Back at home, she ran a hot bath and opened a Corona. In front of the mirror, she stripped, satisfied that there was no physical reminder of her ordeal. She'd have to make a quick trip to the hairdresser sometime soon—the roots were starting to show. Stepping into the warm water, she sat back and reached for the beer bottle. She cursed Rhonda for talking her into a decision that would drive up the hairdresser costs for months to come, an unwelcome reminder of a bad idea. Ellie took another sip, thinking of what Jordan had told her about the victim, and decided not to fret about hair color.

Going over the day in her mind, she wondered what Sergeant Bristol would have to say about Jordan's offer. She figured he didn't have to know about words spoken in private, or whatever else was in the air.

With a sigh, she leaned even deeper in the water. A few weeks ago, she would have walked away, stayed out of the guaranteed trouble of hooking up with someone already taken. Somehow, Jordan had gotten into the path of her newly found attitude to life. The thought made her body tingle all over. She closed her eyes, but a heartbeat later, she jumped, on the verge of sliding into a dream with a dark shadow hovering over her. At least she hadn't dropped the bottle—the last thing she needed was another mess to clean up.

She wasn't going to beg, Ellie promised herself. She'd already walked the line by demonstrating her displeasure with today's assignment, and her eagerness to help out with the detectives' urgent case. The next move had to come from Jordan, which meant she had to make a decision about how much she valued her relationship. Going for someone willing to cheat might not be the best strategy, but Ellie wasn't looking for a long-term relationship. She wanted to feel good again, at home in her body, if only for a little while.

Chapter Two

After waking in a cold sweat for the second time, Ellie decided she had enough and got out of bed at 4:37 a.m. *Bright and early enough for you, Detective?* She hadn't meant to, but she had already changed habits. For the longest time, she'd wear heels in the morning on her way to work and change back into them after her shift. Lately, the sound of heels on the pavement made her uncomfortable. She knew it would abate with time. Why not hurry the process along? They might not be able to catch the bastard who had jumped her, but if she could assist catching the killer Jordan and her team were after, it would go a long way towards making her feel safer again.

Determined, she slipped into a pair of pumps. Sometime this week, she might even go out with her friends again. If Jordan told her no another time, to hell with her. Ellie would have no problem finding someone else in her pursuit of pleasure.

Jordan wore jeans and a white buttoned-down shirt this morning. Ellie had little time to admire her, because they dove into the disturbing reality of the case on the table right away.

"The common theme here seems to be some relationship trouble. This is one thing we know about all the victims so far, a recent breakup. Two of the women straight, one lesbian. The question is where does he find them? Lori Gleason told me she found dates in a chat room. She signed up after her divorce."

11

Ellie had done her best to get herself up to date with the facts. Gleason was currently recovering in the hospital. Isabel Hayes' body had been found behind a dumpster five weeks ago, and the first victim, Eleanor Campbell, had been discovered by trespassing teenagers. The trespassing became rapidly irrelevant, and the high school kids had been taught the lesson of a lifetime in what could happen if you walked into a creepy abandoned building.

"How can we be so sure it's the same killer?" Jensen asked. "I imagine Hayes would not hang out in the same chat room, for obvious reasons."

Ellie could see the hint of indulgence on the detectives' faces. Jordan, however, addressed the question. She pointed to Hayes' crime scene photo.

"You better hope there aren't more like him out there. The victims' injuries are consistent. The rope fibers match. You are right insofar as their life circumstances were different. Gleason preferred the chat room. Isabel Hayes preferred bars. Eleanor Campbell, as far as we know, was the only one in a committed relationship, but the husband's alibi checks out."

"He hates women. Sexually active women. Maybe he got rejected." Ellie didn't realize she'd said this out loud until all eyes were on her. She shrugged. Ellie had done a lot of reading on why some men hated on women, from her undergraduate days on. A lot of those theories had come back to her lately.

"That's a possibility." Jordan's reaction was rather reserved. "It's all theory at this point. What we need is to find the link between all those women. They lived in different neighborhoods, but within a relatively small distance. He's probably local, can't or won't travel. I want you to concentrate on the dates from the chat room so far. We have the data from Lori's computer, every date, every conversation. Look closely for anything suspicious."

"What about Gleason's ex?" Jensen inquired.

"He's coming back from a business trip in Europe. I expect him this afternoon. Meanwhile, let's hope Lori will remember more."

Ellie got up but waited until everyone was beginning their own work. Two of the other detectives left. Jordan, sensing her hesitation, came over to her.

"Lori Gleason...was she raped?" Ellie asked. She hated how all of a sudden, her voice sounded small.

"The rape kit came back negative." Jordan's tone was calm and detached, but there was concern in her gaze. They both knew that left a lot of other possibilities. "Will you be okay?"

"Yes, of course."

"Okay then. Go find the perfect match online."

Ellie couldn't help it, even the probably innocent suggestion brought heat to her face, and lower regions. What kind of person did that make her? They had a job to do, because some women had suffered far worse abuse than she had, and besides, Jordan had a girlfriend. Reason was not helpful.

"More like a date with the devil," she said lightly. "Thank you. I really appreciate this."

"No problem. You still owe me a beer."

For the next fifteen minutes or so, Ellie kept wondering if she'd really heard her say it. However, her fantasies were certainly not priority. She read pages after pages of emails Lori Gleason had exchanged with potential dates, the tone always ranging from flirty to definitely not safe for work. She felt a bit sick, knowing this was the kind of behavior a man would hardly ever be criticized for. Someone had taken offense, kidnapped, beaten, and cut her, would have killed her if the neighbors hadn't called the police. Because she flirted with men on the Internet? Because she enjoyed dating and possibly, sex? The world was fucked up.

She winced at the suggestion of a threesome, and Lori's response, aware of how easy it was to let one's own sensibilities and boundaries seep into judgment. As long as they kept it safe, who was she—or anyone—to blame them?

"My friend would like to join us," Lori had written. *"When can we meet?"* The date had never come to pass, because of Lori's abduction. Unless...Ellie stared at the printout until the letters started blurring in front of her eyes. Of course, two straight people dating and considering a third party was not the same as Isabel enjoying the lesbian nightlife, except to a sexist murderer it might be. Maybe Eleanor's marriage hadn't been that happy after all, and she'd had a secret of her own—they could be looking at a hate crime. Jordan was right. This was a theory, and only one of many possible at this point. They had to stick to the facts.

"I know you've been hurt before, and the same is true for me. I want to meet someone who's committed, who won't let me down. If you can be that person, I promise you won't regret it," said one of the answers Lori had gotten. There might be some people going onto these sites who were honestly looking for a relationship, love. It was hard not to get paranoid. Everybody had something to hide. One of them had sent a poem. Another had promised a trip to an exotic location Lori wouldn't ever forget.

At least Mr. Threesome, with whom the most recent correspondence had taken place, had written emails from his work account. This would be an interesting visit, Ellie thought as she looked up the company, a computer firm, and jotted down the address. The location was right in the center of the circle in which the women had been found.

Jordan, much to Ellie's disappointment, didn't send her and Jensen to talk to Lori's date. Instead, and Ellie realized soon that she was getting the much better deal, she took her to see Lori Gleason. The ride to the hospital was a tad awkward, as Ellie sat straight up, trying not to stare, at Jordan, at her hands on the steering wheel, imagining these hands doing something else instead. She forced herself to keep her gaze straight ahead, focus.

The smells and sounds of the hospital hit her hard. She hadn't been in here since the night she'd been attacked, and the sensory memories put a jarring halt to her inappropriate thoughts.

There was a uniformed officer in front of Lori Gleason's room, greeting them briefly. He confirmed with Jordan that no unauthorized person had tried to approach Lori, and they went inside.

Ellie stopped in her tracks at her first look at Gleason. The instant panic on the patient's face that abated only when she realized her visitors were with the police, the bruises...without a doubt, her injuries were graver than Ellie's had been, but she had a hard time stopping the unwelcome trip down memory lane.

Jordan introduced her to Lori Gleason, and the woman gave a faint smile that slipped from her face so quickly Ellie might have imagined it.

"How are you today, Ms. Gleason?" Jordan asked, keeping her tone soft, non-threatening.

The blank expression, either from medication or self-protection, told Ellie they weren't likely to get a lot of information out of her. Gleason shrugged and winced, the movement causing her pain.

"We reached your ex-husband. He was on a business trip and is coming in today." The news seemed neither helpful nor upsetting for Lori.

"He wouldn't do anything like that. We had a good marriage."

"Why did you get divorced?"

"Am *I* under suspicion for anything?"

Ellie thought to herself that she probably would have reacted the same way.

"No, of course not," Jordan reassured her. "It's important for us to figure out why you were targeted."

"Don't you think I know that? I've been wracking my brain every waking moment. I don't know anymore than I've told you. You probably saw the chats by now. I've had a few dates. Those were decent people, or at least I assumed so. There's nothing else I can tell you."

"I know it's hard," Ellie said, stepping forward. Gleason shot her a suspicious look. She showed emotion, which, Ellie assumed, was better than lethargy. Maybe she knew something that hadn't come to mind yet.

"What do *you* know?"

"I was attacked some weeks ago. Would you mind?" She pointed to the visitor's chair, and Lori shook her head.

"Why are you telling me this? You got away—obviously."

"So did you. I want you to know that it will take some time, but details will come back to you, and that's not a bad thing. It means you'll be able to work through them, now that you're safe."

Lori's expression spoke volumes. At this point, it would be hard for her to believe she'd ever feel safe again. Ellie could sympathize. "I'm sure the last thing you want right now is for us to bother you with questions," she continued. "I hated everyone who asked me about it, I wanted them all to forget about it, so I'd be able to. First of all, I learned it doesn't work that way. Second, we want this man in prison, so he can never hurt anyone else. So, if there's anything you can think of, that comes back to you, please let us know."

"It was dark. He was wearing a mask. I woke up in that basement, and I never saw his face. I'm trying, damn it."

"I know." Ellie suppressed the urge to take the woman's hand. There were situations when touch meant no comfort, on the contrary, it could make a person want to jump out of their skin. "Please know that we're doing everything we can. You beat the son of a bitch already. You lived."

Due to a coincidence, but still. Ellie had the uncomfortable feeling that the woman was able to read her mind. They both had been lucky to benefit from the quick thinking and kindness of strangers. What did it mean? The world wasn't ever safe, no matter how much you tried to prepare for the worst.

"Did they get him?" Lori asked, startling her. "The guy who attacked you, was he arrested?"

Ellie was tempted to lie to her, but she thought the woman deserved better. "No." Lori's face fell. "Which doesn't mean anything for your case. He left traces, people like that make mistakes. We'll catch him. I promise."

"You exchanged a few emails with a guy named Graham Chambers, is that right?" Jordan's interruption was rather abrupt. "You mentioned a friend who would be interested in joining you on that date? Is that something you did on a regular basis?"

"Sometimes," Lori said, defiantly. "What do you want from me? I let you dissect my private life, and I understand why you're going there, but you know what? I don't need that tone from you. I didn't deserve this."

"Nobody does. Can you give us her name?" Jordan was less fazed by the accusation than Ellie which spoke of her experience. Now was not the moment to let the mind wander.

"Sure, though I have no idea how that could help you. We kept it discreet. I hadn't seen her in some time. Her name is Bella Prince. We met at the All Colors."

If Jordan was surprised at this announcement, she didn't let it show. The name of the club told you all you needed to know—everyone was welcome to hook up whichever way, as long as they were adults and on the same page.

"Thank you, Ms. Gleason. Like Officer Harding here said, we look at every detail. Your lifestyle is nobody's business other than yours and that of the people involved, but you caught someone's attention."

"You mean someone's been watching me for some time? Great. What makes you think he'll let this go?" She gave herself the answer. "I take it back. I don't want to know."

"There'll be an officer in front of your door at all times—" Jordan interrupted herself as the doctor came in.

"I think this conversation has been long enough," he said in a rather conversational tone. "Ms. Gleason needs her rest."

"This is all for now," Jordan confirmed. "Thank you. If there's anything else, have Officer Morrison call us."

She didn't say a word until they were halfway back to the station. Ellie couldn't take it any longer.

"Did I do anything wrong? I thought she might be more open if I shared with her what happened to me."

"You were good until you made a promise to her. That's something absolute, you can't take it back."

Really, that was the problem? "I don't intend to take it back. We will catch him."

"Yeah." Jordan sighed, making Ellie wonder if she had been scrambling for something to criticize. Her own line of questioning hadn't gone so well. "Let's go see Mr. Chambers. We can get something for lunch before Lori's ex is due."

"Are we okay?"

"Don't worry," Jordan said. "We're fine."

Halfway through the talk with a flustered Graham Chambers, Jordan's cell phone rang, and she excused herself. "Lunch is canceled," she whispered to Ellie. "Mr. Gleason arrived. He says he's jetlagged and not particularly happy to meet with the police first thing back home, already threatening with a lawsuit. This is going to be interesting."

"More interesting than this?" Ellie whispered back, and Jordan allowed herself a smile before she continued.

"So, Mr. Chambers, Lori Gleason was the only potential date of yours who agreed with your preferences?"

"Oh God, it's so horrible this happened to her," he said nervously. "This will be just between us, right? My wife cannot know about this."

Ellie had caught a glance at the picture frame when they walked into his office, a blonde woman and a boy of about three or four years. Chambers' marriage was the least of anyone's concerns at the moment, but Jordan assured him anyway.

"Lori was very lucky, considering," she said. "We are not investigating you, but we need to talk to everyone who might help us find who targeted her specifically."

"I never even met her. I really don't know much about her other than the emails we exchanged, and the fact that you're in my office now tells me it was a bad idea."

Neither of them laughed, so he moved on. "Anyway. She said she'd bring her friend, and we'd meet at that club, something with...Colors?"

"All Colors," Jordan provided. "That was in her email."

"Yes, but she didn't show up." He sighed. "I guess now we know why. When you see her, please tell her I am so sorry."

"What were you doing on June 6th, around 10:00 a.m.?" Ellie remembered that detail from Lori's file. The security camera of a coffee shop had picked her up that morning, the last time she'd been seen before her abduction. She never made it to work to start her noon shift, but Lori Gleason couldn't explain how she'd come to wake up in a dark basement, tied up.

His eyes widened. "Wait, I thought you said you weren't investigating me..."

"Just a formality." *For now*, rang unspoken.

"Okay, well...the 6th. Wait a minute." Chambers leafed through his calendar, frowning at an entry. "Right. That day. I was meeting with clients all day," he said, uncomfortable. "I can give you their names if you want."

"That would be helpful," Jordan said.

"Look, when Lori didn't show up, I assumed she had changed her mind. I tried to contact her a couple of times, she never emailed me back. I let it go and made arrangements with another woman to go on a date. What was I supposed to do?"

Ellie suppressed a snort. Trying to fix his marriage seemed to have never crossed Chambers' mind. He was a player, but the fantasies he was chasing appeared mild in comparison to the murderer's.

"I understand. You didn't want to waste any time." Jordan said. To her credit, it didn't even sound a bit sarcastic.

"Exactly." He handed her a list with names. "These are the ones I met on the 6th. I need to ask you for discretion though."

"Of course." This time, there was a hint of it in her voice. "Thanks for your time, Mr. Chambers. We'll be in touch."

❧

"Tell me, what's your impression?" Jordan asked when they were back in the car.

My impression is that you're hot when you're putting on pressure. Aware that it would sound crazy unprofessional, Ellie kept her first thoughts to herself. After all, Jordan had asked for her take on Chambers, not on her interrogation or other skills.

"First of all, they're a strange combo, Gleason and Chambers, but hey, whatever works. He seems...careless, not even trying hard. I mean the guy works for a computer firm, and he doesn't cover up his tracks? It was too easy to find him. I'm not sure. He might tie people up on occasion, but I have a hard time seeing him as the killer. These things take planning, right?"

"Right, but not all of them are organized," Jordan reminded her.

"You worked a lot of those cases?"

"A couple." By now, she had learned to gauge from Jordan's expression when she was about to overstep a boundary, but Ellie was too curious for her own good.

"Wow," she said. "That must have been tough. So, you learned a lot about assholes like him, what drives them?" Much like the reading she'd been doing herself.

"My...partner is with the FBI. A profiler."

"Oh." Ellie realized she didn't really want to hear a lot more on the subject. She wondered about Jordan's hesitation to pick a term for her relationship. At a certain age, "girlfriend" might sound too juvenile, "partner," however, had a neutral, business-like ring to it that in Ellie's opinion, didn't work well to describe a loving commitment. Well, maybe this one wasn't so loving. She didn't dare ask. "That's interesting. Are you going to the All Colors today, to ask around?" The change of topic was abrupt, but Jordan went with it, making Ellie think that she might not want to talk any more about her partner either. How long had they been together? Were they not thinking of marriage now that it was legal? Why was she even wondering?

"We'll deal with Mr. Gleason first, but yes, the All Colors is definitely on the list, to see if anyone can confirm what Chambers said. Have any plans tomorrow night?"

They had arrived on the department's parking lot, and Jordan turned to her, waiting for an answer. That moment, Ellie could see the future rather crystal clear. Based on what she'd just witnessed, she was in trouble. Apparently, Jordan could brush aside the subject of her relationship easily. In her question was an unmistakable double entendre. This was wrong, even if both of them wanted it.

Ellie had no illusions. If Jordan had asked her to make out with her right here in the car, she might have said yes. Jordan Carpenter was tough, she had to be to make it where she was now. Without a doubt, that part of her was attractive to Ellie. At a closer look, Jordan had a startling vulnerability about her that she found irresistible. If she needed someone to hold her, Ellie wanted to be that person, among other things.

"Ellie?"

"Yes, sure. I mean no. I don't have plans. What do you want me to wear?"

Something would have to give. She wasn't sure she'd survive the week otherwise.

<hr />

"Mr. Gleason, thank you for coming in. Derek, how about you take a break?" Jordan advised the other detective. Derek Henderson joined Ellie in the observation area, nodding to her before he turned his attention back to the two-way mirror.

Gleason was sweating, and angry. "Ma'am—Detective, could you tell me what's going on here? I'm between flights when I'm hearing that my ex-wife was kidnapped. I do everything I can to help you, come here right after I set foot on the ground, and you're treating me like a suspect! I want to talk to my lawyer, now."

"I don't think there's a need for that at this point, but of course you can. I'm sorry if there was a misunderstanding. We needed to follow up with a potential witness and ran a little late." Jordan's voice was warm and seductive. "I can have my colleague get you something to drink if you want."

"No. I want to get this over with. No one is telling me anything! Is Lori...will she be okay?"

"Lori is safe, don't worry. You came back from Spain today?"

"I told Detective Henderson already. I came straight from the airport. My suitcase is even still in the trunk of my car, if you want to check that."

"Thanks so much for your cooperation." Jordan leaned towards him. "We checked something else though. There's no record of you flying into or coming from Spain."

Ellie's jaw dropped.

"That's odd, wouldn't you say?"

Gleason looked startled for a moment, but he caught himself. "That's odd indeed. There must be a mistake. Besides, I know what you're thinking. Lori and I had a good relationship, even after the divorce. I encouraged her to go out—as I did during our marriage. We had an open relationship. At some point, we drifted apart, and we decided we should end it. We're still friends."

"You didn't mind she was meeting other men, and women?"

"Why would I? I've had my share."

Jordan let the silence linger. Gleason returned her gaze with a cordial smile, but underneath the table, he was tapping his foot on the floor nervously.

"She's good. Pay attention, you can learn something."

Henderson's jovial tone amused her. Ellie was paying close attention to everything that was happening in the room. He had no idea how close.

"Okay. There's still the matter of your flight. You are not on any list. Did you think we wouldn't find out?"

"I told you, they must have made a mistake, and there's no way you can hold me on this. I'm not going to talk to you any longer, and I want to call my lawyer right now. He will tell you the same. This is ridiculous."

23

"All right. Just one more question. Do you know either of those women?" She laid a picture of Eleanor Campbell in front of him. He actually took his time to study it, then shook his head. "Not that I can remember, no."

"This one?"

"No."

"Are you sure?"

Ellie had noticed it too, a minute reaction, a small flinch before he denied. So had Detective Henderson.

"I don't know either of these women, and you are starting to tread on dangerous ground, legally speaking."

Jordan put the pictures back into the folder. "Thanks for the advice, Mr. Gleason. Please, make that call now."

Without a doubt, she'd be in for another long night. Usually, Ellie was good at distancing herself, not letting the workday seep into her off time, but her recent experiences had shaken her boundaries. The crime scene photos, Lori Gleason torn between fear and anger, wondering if she'd ever sleep through a night again, the thought of what could have happened—all of it hit too close to home. Never mind the still unanswered question.

At 11:00 p.m., Ellie wandered around her bedroom, trying to figure out what would be the right outfit for going to All Colors with Jordan. Probably no girls' night out gear, she thought, faintly disappointed. Asking around was not the same as being undercover, and Jordan hadn't mentioned anything of the kind. For a moment, she allowed herself the idea that they might have to play a couple, flirting, kissing...no. That was unlikely to happen tomorrow.

What happened to taking what she felt life owed her?

Ellie lay down on her bed, staring at the ceiling. She was so tired. She had gotten her wish, working upstairs, but if she was honest, she'd wish it could have been any case but this. Masked men lurking in the darkness to prey on someone they considered vulnerable, whom they had been watching, probably for weeks—it was too depressing a thought. There had been no other attacks reported. Maybe he had given up. Maybe he was just waiting, like the man Lori Gleason had escaped from.

Chapter Three

"He's got something to hide." Jordan was still frustrated due to the dealings with Gleason's lawyer the previous day. Indeed, a lack of alibi didn't look so good, but there was no way yet to tie him to the rope fibers or the locations where any of the women had been found. Ellie watched her pace the confines of the office, wishing she had anything useful to contribute. She couldn't imagine a reason why Gleason would fake a business trip in the first place, when he knew it would come out the moment they checked passenger lists. Unless it was never meant to function as an alibi, and his secret was unrelated to Lori's abduction. Ellie realized she had tumbled into a world that was completely alien to her. She liked to go out, flirt, test the boundaries, but chat rooms, open relationships and threesomes were not something she had envisioned for herself.

"Nothing on the couple that bought the house?"

Jordan shook her head. "Upstanding citizens, excellent credit, have never gotten in trouble with the law. They didn't even know there was a trap door. Apparently, it had been covered with a rug when they were visiting. Damn it!"

Ellie flinched though she felt the same, restless, angry. It seemed like the investigation had come to a halt, when the perpetrator they were looking for might have set his eyes on the next victim.

She got up to join Jordan at the board, once more forcing aside her visceral reaction to the gruesome photographs.

That could have been me.

Where the hell did that come from?

Location. Eleanor Campbell. The office building, abandoned. Lori Gleason, another soon-to-be-occupied empty house. How did the killer know? Was he about to move Lori to another place, or kill her there, in the new owner's basement? It was like trying to put together a giant puzzle with only a handful of pieces at the time. Her gaze wandered back to Isabel Hayes. Unlike Eleanor (almost four weeks) it had been only about ten days between the date she went missing, and the driver of the garbage truck had had the worst start into his workday ever. The intervals had gotten shorter. Lori's ordeal had ended on the eighth day.

Lucky.

"He leaves them alone for long hours a day, probably has a day job, stalks potential victims in bars and maybe, chat rooms. How does he choose them?"

"Good question," Jordan said. "I hope tonight we get a bit closer to answering it. As for your question, casual clothes will do. I'd like to show around some pictures...it might help if we don't scream cops at first sight."

"I'm okay with that."

"How are you holding up?" Jordan asked, only for Ellie to overhear.

"It's my job. I'm fine."

"Fortunately," Jordan cast a quick glance at the board behind them, "this is not part of the everyday job. You don't ever get used to it, and it would be bad if you did. You just came back from something horrible."

"I'm aware of that. It sucks. The department shrink told me all about it, but I still thought I might be smarter about it, get over it." Ellie caught herself. "It is what it is. Once we're off duty, would you like to take me up on that beer you said I owe you?"

"Why not? Although, you know that was a joke, right?"

Ellie held her breath for a moment, before Jordan said, "You could come to my place instead. It's not that far from the All Colors."

They had a crime to solve. Ellie kept the thought at the forefront of her mind, though she couldn't deny the excitement when she entered the club with Jordan. Even on a weekday night, it was packed with the hopeful and the hunters, few of them sober. If that had been the objective, they could have probably made a few easy drug related arrests. Tonight, their hope was to connect a few of the loose puzzle pieces. Lori. Chambers. Bella.

Gleason, and maybe a tie to the other women. If they could identify the killer's hunting ground precisely, they were one step closer to identifying him. He wasn't a ghost. Somebody had to have seen the women with him.

Another thing Ellie became soon aware of, were the curious, and in some cases, jealous, looks that followed them. Jordan seemed oblivious or plain used to it, but Ellie returned each of them with a smug smile.

She wondered if Jordan's girlfriend was working out of headquarters, and if she was away often—often enough to bring another woman to their home. Did they even live together? She was about to find out.

The bartender, a blonde with tattooed arms, shook her head regretfully when Ellie showed her the picture of Eleanor Campbell. "Doesn't seem like the right clientele for the place," she mused out loud. "Is that all?"

At the sight of Lori Gleason's photograph, her eyes went wide. "That's the girl they found in the basement, right? I read about it in the paper. I was wondering when you might come by. She was here a few times."

"Do you remember who was with her? Did she go home with anyone?"

The young woman looked uncertain. "You know, the faces blur after a while. There were a few guys, but mostly she was with this other chick, what's her name...Bella. That's all I know. They had a few drinks, danced, whatever else, don't ask me."

"How about this one?"

"You've got to be kidding me," the bartender said when Jordan laid the picture of Hayes in front of her. "You didn't know?"

"Didn't know what?"

"That's Bella!"

Isabel. Bella. Ellie wanted to slap her hand against her forehead.

"Is she okay? In the paper, they said there was only one woman in that basement...oh my God. The others are dead?"

"I'm afraid so," Jordan said. "If you can remember anything about either of them, who they met, who they left with, please, let us know."

"Of course. Why don't you wait for a bit? Sheila will be here in half an hour. She's been here longer than I have, and she works most of the weekends. Maybe she can help you more."

Ellie cast a questioning look at Jordan and got a nod in return.

"Thank you. We'll wait."

For the next thirty minutes, there was nothing to distract them, from the atmosphere around them, the pounding music, the people seeking and finding a connection that might not last longer than tonight. Hope, desire, with a dash of danger. Ellie caught Jordan's gaze on her, speculative. She was all too aware of the heat coursing through her body, pooling between her legs.

Life owed her. Jordan owed her, for all the times she looked at Ellie with that undisguised want in her expression. She wished they could have a drink, take the edge off inhibitions and guilt, but of course that was impossible. Later. If there actually was a later.

Sheila came in earlier than expected, fortunately, and she confirmed her colleague's observations. She had something to add though.

"There was this guy, one time, tall, good-looking, salt and pepper hair, early fifties maybe. I don't know his name."

It didn't sound like Chambers at all, but it wouldn't be surprising that a killer on the prowl had altered his appearance, Ellie thought as she listened to Sheila.

"They were talking, and Isabel seemed pretty pissed afterwards," the bartender continued. "She left early. I haven't seen him since." She looked apologetic. "I'm sorry, but I'm not sure I'd recognize him. Bella and Lori—that's her name, right?—They kept to themselves mostly."

"Can you think of anyone who might have seen something?" Jordan kept her tone as light and relaxed as it possibly could be, given the subject, but her tense composure revealed her frustration, at least to Ellie. Hopefully she'd let her do something about it. Sheila surveyed the crowd thoughtfully. "You might have more luck on the weekend, with one of the regulars."

"One more thing. A guy, blond, around forty, uses the same dating website to hook up with women and couples."

"Oh, you mean Graham? He was here on the night of the fifth, hooking up with someone. They left together. If you want my impression, he's harmless, but a lousy husband."

"Okay. Thank you," Jordan said and turned to Ellie. "I think it's time to call it a night. Come on." Ellie didn't need any more prompting.

Yes, she had known where this would lead all along, probably from the moment Jordan had given her the once over at the bar. Ellie remembered her gaze traveling up her legs, pausing a bit around the neckline of the low-cut top, meeting her eyes with an inviting smile.

Ellie had burned those clothes once she got them back from evidence. She wouldn't let the sorry excuse for a man burn anything else in her life. She'd managed to hold Jordan's interest as well. She was excited, and curious. She was finally feeling something again that didn't make her want to scream—well, not that way, at least. It had to be a good sign.

When they walked up to the apartment building that housed Jordan's home, she craned her neck, curious. The high rise held several condos that, she assumed, would be as modern on the inside as the outside suggested.

"This is pretty cool," she said. "Did you rent or buy?"

"We rented, but the company wants to remodel the units and sell them by the end of the year. I guess we'll have to make up our minds pretty soon." Jordan's tone made it clear this decision wasn't a priority now. Her use of "we," reminder of the third party, silenced Ellie. She took in the clean and spacious lobby, the elevators. The building had the vibe of a luxury hotel.

"It's nice," she finally said. Jordan shrugged.

"Thanks."

Ellie studied her reflection in the mirror wall, a woman troubled, beyond attractive to Ellie, wearing a substantial weight on her shoulders. This wasn't just about the consequences of what

32

they were about to do, she realized. Ellie had been assigned to the case for a week only, and she could feel the tension in her body caused by the confrontation with those pictures and what they meant, every day. She'd seen her share of violence in her day job, but not every day. There had been silver linings, like the child wandering away in the mall found and reunited with the happy mother an hour later. The accident victim who was saved, the grandmother who miraculously convinced the burglar to give himself up and stay until the police arrived. There were losses. Nothing like this, a criminal deciding he should be judge, jury and executioner to the "crime" these women had committed in his twisted mind. It had to take a toll at some point.

Jordan opened the apartment door, and Ellie couldn't help the "wow" that escaped her. From the granite countertop of the kitchen to the light grey sectional with the red pillows, it looked like something out of a catalogue. Every piece of decoration was tasteful and fit into the surroundings. In the dining area sat a massive wooden table with chairs around it, a modern light fixture overhead.

"You want a beer?" Jordan asked, heading for the fridge.

"Sure. Thank you. That means I owe you two."

Jordan smiled before she opened a bottle for each of them. "Would you like a glass?"

"No thanks. This is fine." Ellie sat on the barstool at the kitchen island, wondering what subjects were left for conversation. She could ask another question about the rent versus buy dilemma, but that would inevitably bring up the subject of the other person living here. It was obvious for someone looking around with a trained eye. She didn't want to talk about the case anymore, at least not tonight. Jordan seemed okay with the silence, and so Ellie drank, faster than she maybe should have.

"Would you like another one?"

Ellie contemplated the question, which was harder than the trivial subject suggested. Jordan was standing close next to her, and when Ellie failed to give her an answer, she reached up to brush a strand of hair back from her shoulder, exposing her neck. Ellie shivered. This was what she wanted, wasn't it? Here it began. She craved the touch of a person who would handle her body with respect. She wanted to do something about that warm, pulsing arousal, but all of a sudden, she wasn't sure if this was the right way to go about it. Jordan kissed her, very softly, before her hands wandered down her shoulders, gently closing around her breasts. Ellie drew a sharp breath.

"Come with me?" Jordan's tone was almost hypnotic, or so it seemed to Ellie. She could detect the uncertainty, the longing, interwoven with the unmistakable heat. If they both felt the same, would that count as an excuse?

In any case, Ellie was glad to escape the picture on the mantel, showing Jordan in the arms of another woman.

They sat down on the side of the bed, kissing with more urgency than before, starting to undress each other. The sound of the zipper of her skirt triggered an unwelcome flash of con-science.

Jordan, sensing her hesitation, sat back, waiting patiently.

"I can't believe I..." No, that didn't sound right. As she was struggling for the right words, Jordan pulled her own shirt back down.

"I'm sorry, I got carried away," she said. "This...it's a difficult time for you. I didn't mean to take advantage."

Ellie shook her head so fast the room was spinning. "No, no, that's not it. It's just that I've never been the other woman. I thought I was cool with that, and it seems that I overestimated myself."

Jordan's expression was pained. "Believe me, you're not taking anything away from anyone. It's hard to break something that's already broken."

This was by far not enough to be a justification, but Ellie decided she would take it. For all she knew, whatever happened, it would all be over once she went back to her division. They didn't owe each other anything.

"I can drive you home," Jordan said. "I didn't even have a sip of anything."

Ellie tugged on her shirt, hard, and the next moment, she was on top of her, letting her feel all of that gorgeous body of hers. Ellie gasped out loud before Jordan's mouth was back on hers, and this was even while they still had most of their clothes on, boding well for the rest of the night. Ellie's skirt came finally down with her panties. She was too impatient and sensitized for the teasing touch of Jordan's fingertips, her hand closing around Jordan's and directing her where she wanted her.

Jordan obliged, fingers spreading the warm wetness and massaging her clit until Ellie was trembling, close. She had almost forgotten how good it felt to be at home in her own body. In the past weeks, she had used mostly work, sometimes food and alcohol, to numb uncomfortable sensations. Here and now, she had undeniable proof that she was still capable of feeling pleasure. Jordan Carpenter turned out to be a good choice after all.

She sat back, gently pressing Ellie's thighs open, then her fingers were back, inside, two, then more.

"You're beautiful," Jordan said. Not that Ellie hadn't wondered what she might look like, her back arching, and her head thrown back, but she didn't mind hearing it. The words themselves felt like an intimate caress, never mind the pressure building, her body tensing sharply. This time, Jordan didn't try to slow her down. She kept up the steady rhythm, skillfully reducing Ellie to quivers and whimpers until she stilled, aftershocks still running through her body.

When Jordan pulled her close, she was satisfied to let her body rest in her embrace, even if it was in another woman's bed. *I'm sorry*, Ellie silently directed at her. *You may judge me if you know what it's like to lie bleeding on the sidewalk, not knowing whether the next blow is going to kill you.*

For once, the haunted look Jordan wore so often was replaced with pure bliss. Ellie licked her lips, aware of the other woman catching her breath. Good. That meant despite the boredom with Rhonda followed by the sheer terror she'd been living with, Ellie hadn't lost her touch either.

She got her second beer after all, then, curled up next to Jordan in nothing but a bathrobe.

"Thank you for staying with me," Jordan said. Ellie regarded her for a moment, appreciating the relaxed and disheveled look one only had after great sex. Great, not just good. It gave her the confidence to tackle a question she'd wondered about the whole time.

"Where is she?"

Jordan flinched a bit, not in an exaggerated way, just enough for Ellie to notice.

"Bethany is at a conference. She'll be back tomorrow night." While Ellie contemplated what this meant for her, if anything, Jordan continued, "I've been thinking about moving out. Not just since today, or last week. I think we're at this point where we should take a break, which, I guess, is always code for something else. I know this sounds like a sad excuse, but it's all I can tell you."

Ellie didn't feel terribly sorry, though she knew this was far from stating that they had any shot at a relationship. The truth was neither of them was ready. That little flare of hope...treacherous and inappropriate.

"I'm a big girl. You don't have to explain."

"I want you to know, I'm not mindlessly sleeping around. I've been...aware of you. I thought about buying you a drink that night." She laughed ruefully, but Ellie, startled, detected something else in her tone.

"That night...You mean when...?"

Jordan tightened her hold. "I wish I had. I know it's irrational, and bad shit happens to good people all the time, but still."

"It's over."

"Not until we catch him."

"Great job ruining a perfect night by reminding me the asshole is still out there." Ellie jumped to her feet, started pacing. "Do you know I never walked that way by myself again? I hate this. I hate him."

"You have every right to—and it's probably wise to be careful."

"Careful is great. I'm sick of being terrified." She had to be cautious, or she'd be coming close to a confession that was way too early to make, for either of them. While the chemistry between them might be undeniable, they had also used each other. That was undeniable too. "There's no point," Ellie concluded. "We might never catch him. I can't let my life revolve around this. Besides, we have other things to worry about." That other case was one thing—or the fact that *Bethany* was returning tomorrow. All of a sudden, Ellie felt a surge of jealousy, thinking that come tomorrow, the other woman would stake her claim.

Only that was irrational, because, as Ellie had so eloquently stated earlier, she was the other woman in this equation.

"I want you so much, it's driving me crazy."

She must have said it out loud too because Jordan's eyes darkened at the blunt admission.

"Don't worry. You have me." *For tonight only*, rang unspoken, but Ellie could work with that. She didn't have any other choice.

⁂

Another night, the same procedure. Lori Gleason dreaded being awake, just as much as she dreaded being asleep with the assistance of medication. Some help that was when every time, she was inevitably dragged back into her worst nightmare.

The basement, blackness, the angry voice of a faceless man—and pain. She knew the police didn't mean to put this much pressure on her, but she felt like the sole responsibility was on her, to make her brain work, to remember something she wanted to forget, to help them stop him. She was sick to her stomach thinking that he might do it to other women—that there were others before her, who hadn't survived. She wanted to help put this animal where the sun didn't shine, but she didn't know how. Whatever came back to her was like a code to crack, only fragments.

With all the pain pills and sleeping aids, she often wasn't sure what was real, and what was part of her overactive, hyper-alert imagination. Falling. Pain, again. The sound of the sliding doors of a van falling shut. The hours, the paradox of boredom and terror, waiting for him to come back, knowing that he wasn't going to let her go, even if she promised to be better.

Lori cringed, wondering if she had told that to the detective who had first taken her statement. She didn't remember all of that either. Was it important? The woman officer, Harding, had said every detail was important. This one—probably not important enough to have the officer standing guard call her in the middle of the night.

He'd never planned to let her live anyway. She closed her eyes, trying to block out the noise on her mind, as usually, failing. It went on even after she slipped into a troubled sleep, interrupted by random intervals of darkness and silence, just like in that creepy place. Lori was afraid of bugs, and sometimes, the ghost sensation of fabric or hair brushing against her skin made her jolt awake, her heart racing. Silly she should be more afraid of such a small creature when she was held captive by a man who had broken her arm and promised to keep hurting her until she understood. The scream, the breathlessness, waking in a cold sweat. Always the same.

"If you promise to be good, I might let her live." She could hear the soft whimper.

Her?

With a shaking hand, still only half awake, Lori reached for the call button, before the doubts crept in and she'd change her mind, believing this was all in her imagination. When the nurse came rushing in, she asked her to go and get the officer who was standing guard. Outside, the day was dawning.

Chapter Four

E llie had declined breakfast, but let Jordan talk her into a cup of coffee. It was still dark outside. Neither of them felt much like sleeping any longer. At least, Jordan reflected, this wasn't as painfully awkward as she'd feared. They'd go back to working together, as long as Sergeant Bristol would lend Ellie to the unit. That was priority. All else...Jordan was as much at a loss as she'd been before, but perhaps she should look into finding another place. As the guilty party, she owed Bethany that much, and most of the furniture and décor had been her choice anyway. Bethany cared about appearances.

She wasn't feeling too crappy yet, but Jordan knew without a doubt, the emotion would come, sooner or later. You could say it took two to ruin a relationship. She was doing her part, wasn't she? She cast a quick look at Ellie, feeling a guilty, pleasant wave of affection for the younger woman. Ellie had been beaten, but she refused to stay down. She might be a tad reckless and ambitious, but her record suggested she was an excellent cop who cared about her job and the people she'd sworn to serve and protect. She reminded Jordan of a younger version of herself. Jordan almost laughed at her line of thought. Ego tripping, much? She liked working with her. Ellie was smart and intuitive. She had caught Jordan's eye the first time she'd noticed her during roll call, at the bar, and finally having her had been so much better than Jordan had imagined. Flattery, in words and every one of her looks, didn't harm either.

Ellie had gathered her coat and purse. She walked over to Jordan and kissed her on the cheek. "I'll see you tomorrow?"

"Yes. Of course."

Jordan turned her around, cupping her face in both hands. Their kiss might feel like desperation, but it was possibly also the last one, in a while, or forever.

When the door fell shut behind Ellie, she stood in the same spot for almost a minute before she turned to the bedroom. She should have so much decency as to wash the sheets before Bethany returned. What would happen after that, she wasn't sure.

Bethany was back early, much earlier than Jordan had expected her.

"Hey, honey, I'm home."

For the life of her, Jordan couldn't determine if her words were meant to be sarcastic, even though they sounded friendly enough. So much for her detective skills. Then again, Bethany had always found a way to outwit her instincts—maybe they taught you that in profiler school.

"Hi. Did you have a good trip?"

She studied the woman who had shared her life and bed for the past nine years. No, that description didn't seem to fit. What they were in each other's lives could better be said with a term like guest, or maybe hostage.

Bethany, as usual, looked impeccable even after the four-hour flight. She claimed to never suffer from jet lag. It was all in the mind and habits—except when she was a bit more short-tempered and frustrated after those trips. She could meet someone, someday, at one of those conferences. That wasn't like Bethany though. She wasn't the cheater. Jordan was.

"Well, you know. As long as it gets me from A to B." Bethany's tone and expression softened. "I missed you."

"I missed you too," Jordan said automatically. Bethany smiled as if she'd just won an argument, and maybe that was an appropriate assessment. They shared a brief kiss before Bethany reached for the handle of her suitcase. "I see there's coffee, good. I just put this away, and we can have breakfast."

"Sure."

Listening to the sound of her walking around in the master bedroom and the adjoining bathroom, Jordan began to set the table, bracing herself. Sure enough, after a few minutes, Bethany returned.

"Laundry day," she remarked.

Jordan wasn't sure if Bethany was waiting for any further explanation, her stomach tensing as she anticipated the exchange of words to come. She tried anyway. "Yeah. I thought I'd get it done before you come back...I expected you later."

"You're not working today?"

"Yes...I will. Later."

This was all Jordan's fault, she realized. This wasn't the first time she felt like a kid who'd been called into the principal's office around Bethany, but of course, this time, she had a reason. She could have walked away years ago. Maybe.

Bethany came to the table, sat. Waiting. Jordan recognized the tactic. She used it herself often enough, in the interrogation room. Here inside their home, the tables were turned on her. Bethany wasn't trying to stare her down though. She was deeply disappointed.

"No. Damn it, Jordan, not again."

Jordan could feel the heat creep up her face. "What are you talking about? You're tired. Why don't you lie down for a bit, and I'll come pick you up for dinner later?"

"Right. Two cups in the sink, you washing the sheets at six in the morning. It's not the welcome I imagined, but why am I even surprised?"

"What's that supposed to mean?"

"Nothing. I don't feel like sleeping," Bethany said. "However, I'm starving. How about toast, could I have some? Can you handle that, Jordan?"

Jordan supposed she deserved that. If Bethany let it go, if they could just not talk about this right now, she'd be okay. The moment she put two slices of bread into the toaster, the phone rang.

"I'm sorry, I've got to get that."

Bethany made a dismissive gesture, and Jordan picked up.

"Detective, it's Officer Morrison. Lori Gleason says she remembers more details. There might have been another woman with her."

"Oh f—" Jordan held back the expletive, for whose sake, she wasn't sure. Mostly, it was because it wouldn't serve anyone. "I'll be right there."

To Bethany, she said, "I need to go."

"Sure you do," Bethany said indulgently, taking a sip of coffee.

"Look, this woman has been through hell."

"It's fine. Go. I can make my own breakfast and operate the dryer."

"Thanks." Somewhere between closing the door behind her and starting her car, Jordan made the transition from her desolate private life into her work persona. She needed to focus. The clock had started to tick faster.

Lori was crying, apologizing, as if the other woman who might or might not be still alive was her responsibility. In some strange way, that line of thinking gave her the illusion she might be able to control something, anything...Jordan thought it was becoming hard to draw the line between the two of them—the victim who survived, and the investigator expected to solve the case. If they, God forbid, found another body, who *would* be responsible?

She couldn't fathom the idea. She couldn't fail. Jordan had almost resigned to the fact that she wasn't very good at handling her life. She relied on the job being the one thing she was good at, but now there was a woman out there, whose chances of surviving were diminishing by the minute. Had she been kidnapped before Lori? That wasn't good. If he'd taken her after, it meant he was getting bolder.

"I remember more of it now," Lori said, her voice hoarse with tears and despair. She was hanging on by a thread. "He was talking crazy, like all of this was some sort of training. He'd spare her if I succeeded, but I never knew what he wanted from me!"

"Relax, it's okay. You're safe now." Jordan wasn't sure if her words were a comfort to anyone, let alone the distraught woman, but she had to try. "Was that the only time you heard the woman? Do you think she was in the same room?"

"Close by. I think he brought her in. Did you find the collar?"

Jordan, taken aback, searched Henderson's gaze, and he shook his head. For a moment she wondered if they'd come here in vain, that the other woman, and everything else, might be a product of drug-induced nightmares.

"What collar, Lori?" she asked softly.

"Didn't you find it? He made me wear it, real tight. He said he'd make it tighter every time I didn't learn. I could never figure out what the damn lesson was!"

Training. Lesson. Without a doubt, there was some significance in that. Jordan wasn't too sure about the collar. All the victims had shown bruises in the neck area, but the place where Lori had been kept was pretty bare. Something didn't add up. She'd figure it out, she always did, but until then, it would be driving her crazy, especially knowing that lives depended on her making the connection. This perp was just getting started, and he wouldn't stop until they caught him.

"We'll follow up on that, Lori, I promise." She thought of something else. The All Colors wasn't quite the venue for this audience, but maybe Lori and Bella—Isabel—had known more. After a moment of contemplation, she asked Derek to leave, hoping Lori might be more comfortable answering her question. Ellie should be here. She seemed to have formed a good rapport with the woman. Ellie, however, wasn't fleeing her home on a Sunday morning.

"Lori, did you and Bella ever look for partners in the BDSM scene?"

She shook her head. "Believe me, it's not what you're thinking. It wasn't our thing, but we had some friends...There was no safe word for me in that basement. It doesn't work that way." Jordan thought some more research might be in order, but she trusted that Lori had a different kind of expertise in that area. However, he could have been some imposter, involving S/M elements in his fantasies. "What about your ex-husband?"

Lori looked angry and frustrated. Jordan couldn't blame her. Having her private life dissected for everyone's scrutiny and judgment after the trauma she'd been through had to be beyond trying. She waited, and Lori gave a sigh that sounded close to a sob.

"I know you have to ask these questions, and I pray you find the other woman, but...I don't know how much longer I can take this. Our sex life wasn't so different from that of millions of others. Who does he think he is?"

"We'll find out."

"Wait. You didn't hear anything about Bella, did you? We weren't best friends, but I thought she might come to see me if she heard."

Jordan shook her head. Sometimes, a lie was indeed the merciful solution. The comfort of cowards, maybe. Then again, this wasn't for Jordan's comfort. She didn't want to unleash yet another trauma on Lori, and she needed her focused and alert.

Dealing with the missing persons database, as usual, made it hard not to lose said focus herself, too, too many stories, too many fates uncertain—the youngest, a girl of three years. She was looking for someone who fit the profile, a woman roughly between her late twenties and early forties, attractive by societal standards, single or divorced, dating, a resident of the area circles within the map that Lori had helped establish.

Judy Lawrence, age thirty-one, reported missing by her sister Meg, caught her eye. Judy, recently divorced, had moved in with her sister while she was looking for her own place. Lori: June 6th. Judy: June 26th.

"What is it?" Derek asked. She hadn't realized she'd covered her mouth with her hand until he spoke to her. It could be a complete coincidence. There could be a relation which would come with unforeseen consequences. It had been the 16th when Ellie was attacked on her way home. She pulled up the report of the 16th, scanning the pages. A man appearing seemingly out of nowhere. Dark clothes, fit, wearing a ski mask. Jordan shuddered. If those pieces came together, two women had gotten away from him, which meant without a doubt a blow to his ego. There had to be something else they all had in common, something they hadn't seen yet, something that might save Judy Lawrence's life. She went back to the board and the map. The All Colors was well within the circle they had established—so was the area where the elderly woman had called 911 after hearing screams outside her home. The officers first on the scene were third year graduates of Ellie's class. They had called for backup and notified Sergeant Bristol that one of their own had been attacked, by a man not yet apprehended. Time to turn up the heat.

She found Sergeant Bristol in his office, on the phone. He signaled for her to wait, so Jordan did, having a hard time not to fidget.

"Carpenter," he said. "What can you tell me about this other woman?"

"I think we found a match. There's something else I wanted to talk to you about."

"Officer Harding? How's she doing?"

"Doing okay. I noticed something though." She laid the notepad she'd used earlier in front of him. Bristol frowned.

"Three sixes? Is this some strange occurrence, or is he mocking us?"

"I don't know yet. I'm not even sure how Harding fits into this, but if she got away from the same guy, it might explain why he took another woman so soon."

"Here I thought you'd bring me good news for once. Go talk to Harding. You seem to get along well—" Jordan kept a straight face though she felt the blush creep onto her face. "See if she can come up with anything else. I'm not sure yet this is compelling evidence, but I want you both to be careful. Have Henderson follow up on Lawrence."

"Will do, sir."

Ellie looked much too happy to see her when she let Jordan in. "Wow. I didn't expect you," she said, sounding a tad nervous. "Come on in."

"There have been some knew developments. Bristol sent me."

"Oh." Ellie's eyes widened for a brief moment. "Okay. Have a seat?"

"I won't be long. There's something strange about the dates when the women went missing." Jordan could tell that Ellie relaxed slightly. Too early. "The day you were attacked seems to fit right in. We were wondering if there was anything that came back to you. Memory is not always linear when you've been through a trauma," she added, finding that the words had a trivial ring to them. Ellie's expression was guarded now.

"You and the sergeant would probably be the first to know. What is this? Are you trying to find a way to send me back downstairs?"

Not for a minute had Jordan considered this interpretation. Now that it was in the room, she wondered how they could continue to work together given the undeniable attraction. Even with the case accelerating, she could feel it, smoldering under the surface.

"That has nothing to do with us," she said, her tone final. "Lori Gleason claims there was another woman. We are trying to find her before he kills her. The night you were attacked, the date, it's right in the middle of when Lori and Judy went missing. It could be a coincidence, but maybe it's not. Have a look."

Frowning, Ellie regarded the notes Jordan had shown Bristol earlier. "It's just numbers. I thought we established this guy is unorganized, compulsive. Numerology? That doesn't seem to fit. Really, you and Bristol are reading 666 into this? I don't believe this murderer sees himself as the devil. On the contrary, he has the air of a self-righteous asshole." She was talking fast as if to fit as many words in as possible before Jordan could contradict her.

"It's not just the numbers. If the cases are related...Lori got away, and so did you. He's angry."

"We don't know. If there's one thing I've learned this week, it's we don't really know a lot about him. See, I don't think this is...conclusive. Bristol is not taking me off the case, is he?"

The potential for conflict, as if they hadn't created enough of it already, was laid bare.

"Not yet, but you know what this could mean. You're not his average target." Jordan was pretty sure that the term victim wouldn't be welcome. "You got away. You're a cop."

"So, you think he wants to follow up on that? I think with Lori surviving and remembering things, he's got his hands full, if, and that's still a big if, there's any relation."

"We need to consider the possibility."

"I need to feel like I'm worth something!"

There was a moment of terse silence after Ellie's outburst startled them both. "Let me break it down for you. I've been feeling like shit every day since it happened, because I walked home, wearing something that's nice to look at, and I know that's what you were doing that night. However, it wasn't the best gear for when you need to run away. I let this guy jump me. I'm a trained police officer and I...I froze. I needed to take a chance on a little old lady being brave enough to call 911. I'm back though. I can do my job. Don't take this away from me."

Jordan finally accepted Ellie's offer and sat down on the edge of an armchair in the living area. She understood perfectly how Ellie felt, and why she was feeling that way. That was why, at the first sign of proof to her theory, Ellie needed to be off the case, away from the possible scrutiny of a serial killer. "Lori said something about a collar he made her wear. There was nothing like that at the scene, which looked way too clean anyway."

"You think he moved her?"

"Possibly. You know that whatever happens with this case, everyone is on the lookout, right?"

"Yeah, as usual, when it's one of our own. I know."

"It's the truth."

"I'm lucky to have you guys." Ellie sounded a little less re-signed, braving a brief smile. "I also have to prepare myself for the possibility that he's getting away with it. It happens."

Jordan couldn't argue with that. "Okay. I wanted to give you a heads-up."

"Thank you." They both hesitated too long, and then spoke at the same time.

"Good night—"

"Would you like to...stay for a bit?" Ellie asked. There was hardly anything Jordan wanted more at this moment, hide in her arms and forget about all those women-hating fuckers out there. Forget about Bethany who probably hated Jordan, for a more understandable, logical reason.

The memory of Ellie trembling and moaning with pleasure underneath her nearly undid all the fairly good intentions she'd brought with her.

"I was about to order pizza. How about it?"

"I'm sorry. I can't. Bethany came back this morning."

"I see."

"I'm really sorry," Jordan tried again, but Ellie brushed her off.

"No, that's okay. I meant what I said. I need this job." She laughed wryly. "I guess I needed to get laid too, so thanks for helping me out with that. Don't worry, I won't go all *Fatal Attraction* on you."

"Ellie."

"You better go."

So Jordan did, telling herself she had no reason at all to feel hurt. None. Just like the last time, she'd brought this on herself, and just like the last time, nothing would change. Her only chance at slightly redeeming herself was trying to find a man who liked to torture women in basements before killing them.

Jordan didn't feel like facing Bethany yet, so she drove back to the station to see how far Henderson had gotten on Judy Lawrence's case.

⁂

"You're here, good," Derek said. "Have a cup of coffee. Here's some reading for you." At her quizzical look, he explained. "Lori Gleason's blood work. We know he drugged her, but that's some heady cocktail."

Jordan groaned when she read the term hallucinogens. This could mean a serious setback, especially if the higher-ups thought that some of her claims might not be as credible. However, Judy Lawrence's case fit. There was no reason to think the other woman might have been a figment of Gleason's tormented imagination, due to the trauma inflicted on her. Pain killers. Muscle relaxants. She wasn't kidding herself. It didn't mean the perp had had second thoughts. He'd been drawing out the finish for as long as possible. So he wasn't that unorganized, had planned enough to get his hands on a multitude of drugs, tools, locations. If Lori had been moved to a house about to change owners in a matter of days, where had she been held before?

Pins on a map. She was dreaming of this map at night, her subconscious struggling to find the missing link. Jordan knew it was there.

"Anything new from Harding?" Henderson asked. She shook her head.

"I talked to Lawrence's sister," he said. "She said the exact same thing that's already in the report. They fought because Judy partied a lot rather than looking for a new job and apartment. Meg, the sister, even made an appointment with a realtor for her, but Judy never went."

"She didn't tell you where Judy was going to party?"

"Well, that's the only interesting part. Guess: Your favorite place. I was thinking we'd drop by on the way home."

"Nothing I'd rather do on a Sunday night," she said.

Jordan felt fairly optimistic when she climbed the stairs to her apartment, a last-minute evasion tactic not to take the elevator. At least the case was moving forward. Lawrence had been another regular at the All Colors, and unlike Lori and Isabel "Bella" Hayes, she hadn't tried to keep a low profile.

"Wow, now I know why he looked familiar. No, he wasn't the guy I saw with Bella and Lori, but he and Judy hung out a lot," Sheila told her when Jordan drove by the bar. She gave Jordan a troubled look. "She's not dead, is she? I'm beginning to think I should get out of here as soon as I can."

Jordan would have liked to reassure her, but too many arrows pointed at the All Colors. Who knew if the killer would distinguish between someone who worked here and those who came to find more than a paycheck?

Tomorrow, they'd lean a little harder on Chambers. He seemed to have a knack for hanging around women who then disappeared. Jordan would have liked Gleason better as a suspect, especially since his business trip was obviously a ruse, but she could live with being not always right with first impressions, as long as she could solve the case. For now, she had to test the waters at home.

"I see you tried your best not to have a single meal with me today," Bethany greeted her. Jordan shrugged and gave her a half-smile, conceding that her assessment wasn't too far off. "I'm sorry. This case is still wide open."

"You don't have to apologize. I had some work to do as well. We can still order in."

"Sure. I'd like to take a shower first."

"Wait," Bethany called after her. "What do you want?"

"Whatever you prefer."

When she returned from the bathroom, Bethany had set the table and poured a glass of wine for each of them. Much as she tried, Jordan couldn't muster the right emotions she knew she should have. The faint sense of guilt came from logical deduction, but she couldn't *feel* it. Too much was already broken between them, had been for a long time. They were treading carefully on broken glass, instead of trying to clean up.

She thought of Ellie, and her parting words, surprised at the instant pain. She was overreacting, for sure. It would be ridiculous to expect more of the young rookie than a one-night stand. Yet, she wished she could be with her right now, for once have an uncomplicated relationship without the entanglements of guilt and obligation.

The doorbell rang, and Bethany got up to answer the delivery guy from the Chinese restaurant. Before they sat down to eat, she filled Jordan's glass once more and leaned close to kiss her. "I hope you didn't open the toy drawer for her," she whispered.

In a strange sense, Bethany seemed to enjoy the situation. Either way, she came out on top.

"We don't have a toy drawer," Jordan said.

"No, but maybe that's something we should look into. If it keeps you from straying, it might be worth it."

Jordan kept her gaze on her plate. "I'm not sure I'm hungry." This, like so many other words spoken, was a lie. She was actually starving, contemplating if going to bed with a rumbling stomach would be slightly more dignified than listening to Bethany.

"No reason to waste perfectly good food. Contrary to what you think, Jordan, I'm not trying to make you feel worse."

"Could have fooled me." She had to stop, not go for the bait.

"Really? How do you think this is making *me* feel?" Obviously, Bethany didn't expect an answer. She sighed. "I know it's not entirely your fault. Things haven't been so great, and I contributed to that as well. I'll try harder. It will be different this time."

Jordan hadn't missed the emphasis. At this point, Bethany wasn't willing to give her any credit for trying. "I can't do this right now. This case is...It's bad. I can't have any distractions."

"Of course." In a heartbeat, Bethany's tone had turned warm and conversational. She reached for Jordan's hand. "When all of this is over, we can take some time for ourselves."

It sounded good in theory, but they'd been there before. After this case, there would be another, and another one after that. In nine years, both of them had become so good at pretending, it was disturbing at times.

They spent the rest of the evening glossing over those heavier subjects. Bethany had some reading to do while Jordan mentally prepared for another visit to Chambers. Probably, she wouldn't take Ellie this time—there'd be enough to do at headquarters. She was still going over the upcoming workday in her mind when Bethany joined her, slipping her robe off her shoulders, and crawled under the covers with her, naked.

You belong in the Victorian era. He snickered at this result of a silly meme, a distraction between clients. Close enough, though he liked the no nonsense rules of the Middle Ages even better. Once a woman was accused of being a witch, the fate that awaited her was worse than a late 1800s' asylum. The general idea was often the same: Women were believed to be ravenous sexual creatures that needed to be controlled at any cost. Come to think of it, they could have learned something from some of today's right-wing politicians.

He wasn't quite so emotional on the subject.

Still, a certain behavior *was* an abomination, and he was more than willing to do his share of cleaning up. Truth be told, he enjoyed it too, even with the snags he'd hit lately. He wasn't feeling threatened at this point. In fact, he was already looking forward to his next project. That was the hardest part, not to get carried away and finish up one obligation before he took on the next. However, at the moment, there was nothing specific on the horizon, and the course of the investigation suggested it might be a good idea to lay low for a while.

He logged out of his account when the doorbell rang. Maybe after this appointment, he'd be inspired.

Chapter Five

S he could feel the sharp pain when the back of her head made contact with the unforgiving concrete, panic rising when her air supply was cut off by the leather collar...Ellie bolted upright in bed, her heart racing. No.

That wasn't what happened. In her nightmare, memory had gotten mixed up with what Jordan had told her about Lori Gleason's statement. Ellie pushed back the covers, shivering as she put her feet on the floor, trying to get her bearings. She could almost smell the leather. Her senses were in overdrive too since the attack. She couldn't fathom what Lori Gleason was going through right now, and frankly, Ellie didn't want to imagine. She was irritated to feel herself tearing up, alone and pitying herself, because her new approach to life wasn't working as well as she'd hoped. What had she expected?

"Oh, shut up," she said out loud when she realized she could come up with answers all too easily. Tomorrow, she'd have to show up at work and forget about everything that happened between her and Jordan. It was for the better. Jordan had never intended to leave her partner, even if for a few brief, foolish moments, Ellie might have imagined this could be in the realm of possibility. They both had bigger problems if Lori was right.

Compared to the woman locked in a dark basement, everyone's problems became relative.

Yet, there was something about piecing together, trying to solve the riddle that intrigued her. Of course, everyone's objective was to put a dangerous man behind bars, bring justice for his victims. Ellie had sensed that kind of atmosphere working closely with Jordan, Derek, and their colleagues. As much as it was their job, it was also a challenge. They were skilled, ambitious and bold, and they answered it.

Ellie knew she belonged there. She would do whatever it took to make her place within this elite group permanent, sometime soon.

Good intentions.

Jordan was already there when she arrived at the station, her stance both distant and apologetic. Ellie could only imagine why, not that she wanted to.

"I'm going to follow up on Chambers," Jordan told her, and, pre-emptively, "You're not being punished. I need someone on the phone here. There's been another alert out for Judy Lawrence, and the phones are already going crazy. Jensen can help you with that."

Ellie shrugged. As much she aspired to become one, she wasn't a detective yet, and if she wanted to work with them, she had to play by their rules. As long as there was a sliver of a doubt whether or not the man in the alley was their killer, she had to lay low.

"Before I go, there's something I need to show you." Jordan had lowered her voice, and that worried Ellie a bit. Did she have any news she needed to break to her gently?

"You can tell me now," she said. "I swear I'm not going to break."

She wasn't sure what to make of Jordan's smile, but Ellie could hardly deny what it did to her. It was much too early in the day for that kind of tingle.

"Come with me. This won't take long," Jordan promised and went ahead. Ellie hurried to keep up with her.

"You didn't make an arrest, did you?" she asked when Jordan opened the door to one of the interrogation rooms. Both the room and the observation area were empty. Jordan caught her off guard by pulling her into the corner next to the observation window for a deep, hungry kiss. Those were hardly the actions of a woman happy at home, Ellie thought, and then she stopped analyzing the situation altogether, letting sensation take over, the heat of Jordan's body pressed against hers, her impatient, wandering hands. Ellie struggled to keep the sounds in. In all the time she'd worked in this building, she'd never once imagined doing anything like it, or how turned on she'd be. This would be over within minutes, for both of them.

Jordan stepped back, catching her breath. Ellie decided she liked very much what she saw. If Jordan wasn't quite begging her with words, her expression and tense stance did. Distance had gone out the window. "I need you."

Ellie was certain this wasn't something people often heard from Jordan, and she wasn't taking it lightly, even though it might not be the best basis for any kind of relationship.

"You're going to work late tonight," Ellie said, the rasp of her voice revealing as to how close she'd come to abandon all reason. "Right? Maybe you'll even have a good reason to drop by my apartment again. You'll have me," she added. The hopeful, almost shy expression on Jordan's face was unlike the woman who, just a moment ago, had been about to ravish her, up against the wall. Even the thought made Ellie flush with sudden heat. Jordan was a woman with many facets, some of them complicated, all of them intriguing. Ellie wasn't ready to let her go yet, not before she had learned each of them.

"Go," she said. "I'll wait for a couple of minutes."

"Don't be late," Jordan said before she left.

When she returned to the conference room, Ellie wished she hadn't been so worried about appearances, because the door was already closed, and she was indeed late. Bristol was present, so were most of the detectives and a woman Ellie didn't know. Given the slight frown on her face, not to mention the suit, Ellie guessed her to be FBI. Some clichés had their merits, and the unhappy glances shared between the detectives further confirmed her theory. She sent Jensen a questioning look, and he shrugged.

"Ladies and Gentlemen," Bristol said, "I'd like to introduce Dr. Roberts, a profiler with the Bureau. There have been some new developments, and Dr. Roberts' expertise will give us a different perspective on what to look for. Which is even more important because Seattle PD has a case with the same M.O."

"What?" At least, Ellie had said it under her breath, but the woman looked her way anyway, her gaze calculating, interested, and then it hit her.

"My partner is with the FBI. A profiler."

What were the odds?

"I take it that so far, you've assumed our boy is local, and that's how he chooses his victims. I happened to attend the autopsy in Seattle, and the details fit. The rope, strangulation marks that are likely from a leather collar. What we know about the victim's..." She paused for a bit, "habits and lifestyle, is similar to your cases here. Apparently, he sees it as something punishable to have more than one sexual partner at a time. On which most people might agree. It's just that we don't go around killing anyone for it."

Nobody laughed, if that had been her intention.

"How do you know it's not a copycat?" Jordan asked, a hint of irritation to her tone. She barely looked at Roberts.

"Seattle has a media blackout on those details, just like you do. Unless somebody has a special friend with the press, no one could know about them."

"I don't believe there's any reason to suggest that." Bristol's tone was calm, but final. Ellie had a hard time keeping herself from fidgeting. Even though most people in the room were bristling with the implied accusation, she still felt like being the unwilling center of attention—that of Dr. Bethany Roberts, anyway.

"Good," Roberts said coolly. "I also understand there's been no arrest made so far."

"One of Lori Gleason's dates was seen with another missing woman. I'm going to see him once we're done here," Jordan explained.

"No luck on Mr. Gleason's alibi?"

"He's been stonewalling," Derek said, coming to Jordan's help. "We don't have anything on him but the lie about the business trip."

"Now you do," Bethany said. "We're not yet sure it was a business trip, but there's a reason why he wasn't in Spain. Seems like he preferred rainy Seattle instead, if his email to the victim is any indication."

Jordan shook her head. "Where is all of this coming from all of a sudden?"

"I'm sorry there was no time to send you the memo, Detective, as this is kind of urgent. I believe you're going to pick him up?"

Jordan jumped to her feet and picked up her coat in curt angry movements before she left the room.

"Chantal was a business partner. Yes, I went to Seattle, we had a meeting, I went on my way. I did not kill her!"

"Why the big secret?" Detective Henderson asked. "Because that really doesn't look too good for you right now." Jordan stood leaning against the wall, her arms crossed over her chest.

"Are you kidding me? You were looking at me from the beginning, with Lori and everything. I have a business to run. I can't have this kind of attention."

"Too bad. You have our attention now. You knew what Lori was up to in those chat rooms, and don't even try to tell us your meeting with Chantal was all professional. There was some code in that email, but we figured out what it meant. The staff at the club recognized you. Rope and leather, go figure."

"You've got nothing," Gleason spat. "That was all consensual. They should have told you that too."

"Then why did she wind up dead?"

"I don't know!"

Ellie had trouble following the conversation. She had somehow managed to sneak in once more, uncomfortable, unable to stay away.

"This must be tough on you," Dr. Roberts remarked.

You have no idea, was her first impulse, before the implications of the woman's statement hit home. Ellie turned to her, wondering if she should feel betrayed, if Dr. Roberts had a sixth sense, or if she was just fishing.

"Coming back to work after an experience like that," the profiler clarified. "You're expected to move on, but there are triggers everywhere you go. I heard about your case. I was curious as to why the sergeant put you on this one."

"The department shri—psychiatrist cleared me," Ellie said which sounded more defensive than she'd hoped. "I'll be taking the detective's exam next year. I can use the experience." She didn't know why she'd added that. It was none of Bethany's business. Ellie's mind was still reeling from the interaction between her and Jordan. Why were they even still together?

"Good for you," Roberts acknowledged. "It never hurts to form...connections early on."

Ellie chose not to answer that and instead direct her attention back to the interrogation, only she had the feeling it was her under suspicion.

⁓

They were back at Jordan's desk discussing what they'd gotten from Gleason, and the steps to take from here.

"You knew. Why didn't you tell me that's why you were in Seattle?" In the course of the long and tiring interrogation, Jordan's anger hadn't abated a bit. Some of it was for a rational reason, she thought. However, it would be a lot harder to sell "working late" to her girlfriend now. Bethany, very much relaxed in an environment where she was not enthusiastically welcomed, sipped her coffee.

"When would I have told you? My boss cleared this with yours. It didn't impact the investigation in any way. If anything, I can help you speed things up a bit."

"Well. Thank you."

"You're welcome." Bethany gave her an indulgent smile. "Come on, don't make that face. It will be like old times, you and me working together."

That was the problem, Bethany was longing for the old times, while Jordan had done what she could to get away from them. The tug of war continued, and Judy Lawrence didn't have the time for their respective sensibilities. Gleason claimed he'd never seen her, and they couldn't prove otherwise. She still thought it might be worth a shot to talk to Chambers again. Bethany's presence was disconcerting to her in many respects, yet she would have to deal with it. Another reason to close this case as soon as possible.

"Yeah. Great."

"He is involved somehow," Bethany said. "It's what your gut will tell you too if you care to listen."

"I need more than that he's looking guilty to you."

Bethany scoffed. "Pretending to go to Spain? Give me a break. He looks fine to me as the unorganized punisher, but let me have a go at him, lay out the possibilities."

"His lawyer will have your hide, and mine too. We can't put him at the scene."

"Not yet." Bethany acted in the professional context much as she did in their private lives—she didn't take no for an answer.

⁂

Too much, too close. Jordan breathed a sigh of relief when she was finally able to lay this workday to rest. Bethany had disappeared earlier, obviously dissatisfied with the D.A.'s assessment of the situation, demanding more compelling evidence. In Seattle, the final test results of the autopsy on Chantal Perron hadn't come back yet. Jordan had fled the scene, trying to make sense of clues that refused to come together.

Two of the crime scenes, Eleanor and Isabel, were within walking distance. Close by was also the All Colors. Lori Gleason's pin on the map was in another part of town in a more residential area. Not far from Ellie's home, Jordan realized. Coincidence? The killer had moved Lori—but how did he pick his locations in the first place? Where was Judy Lawrence?

A couple of blocks from the All Colors, a newer office building towered over its neighbors, the highest floor housing a restaurant and observation deck.

She wasn't even sure what exactly she was looking for, but this was how the image emerged sometimes, looking at the bigger picture, finding out what they had missed.

Women being judged for their lifestyle. Their entertainment centering around chat rooms and one particular venue. Jordan took the elevator up to the observation area, taking out the copy of the map she carried with her. They had checked on the owners of the abandoned office building, the firm who had finalized the sale of the house where Lori had been found, and the buildings around where Hayes' body had been dumped. The real estate firm was here in this tower, actually. They had talked to employees, traced the steps of the sale, but nothing had come up.

Jordan stood in front of the sign longer than she meant to, a thought forming that wasn't related to the case at all. If she went down that road, did it mean defeat? She straightened her shoulders and pulled the door open. She wasn't going to commit to anything, not yet. It wouldn't harm having an alternative.

There was a woman in her fifties behind the desk, looking up with a friendly smile when Jordan entered the office.

"Good evening. How can I help you?" Her choice of words alerted Jordan to the fact that they were probably closing soon, and she might have more questions than could be answered in a few minutes.

"I didn't realize how late it was. I'll come back another time."

"That's no problem," said the man who walked inside through a door from the back. "Liz, you can go home. I'll take it from here." He was a bit younger, dressed in a grey suit that looked crisp despite the late work hour, wearing the same cordial smile as his receptionist. "Let's go over here..." He pointed at his desk. "Detective." His expression turned somber. "We spoke to your colleagues a while ago. I hope this doesn't mean bad news? I recognized you from your picture in the newspaper," he clarified. "Jonathan Darby. Then again, you know that already."

"Jordan Carpenter. I'm sorry for the misunderstanding. This is private. I am thinking about buying a condo, or a house even. Actually, I have no idea what I'm doing, that's why I'm here."

His relief was visible. Jordan could relate. She would prefer to be able not to talk or think about this case for some time either, not that she had the luxury.

"Why don't we sit down, and you tell me what you are looking for? I'm sure you have some idea of what you need in a home."

"Maybe I should come back."

"Don't worry. We don't slam the door in anyone's face, just because it's closing time. Would you mind if I had a coffee though? I could offer you one too. I guess we both had a long day."

"Sure, why not?" Jordan returned his smile, oddly excited about having this little secret all to her own. For now. Until she walked into this office, she hadn't even considered the opportunity, but now she couldn't help thinking what it would be like to settle down in a space that was her own. Without Bethany. Without anyone at this point, because as much as she was attracted to Ellie and couldn't wait to be with her again, she needed room to breathe. Maybe Mr. Darby could provide her with some.

He returned with a small tray, two cups of coffee, milk, and sugar. "I have the suspicion though that you might take it black. Call it a hunch."

"Your hunch is accurate."

"I read about that poor woman," he said. "It's such a relief she's alive. Anyway, have you considered some specifics? A house, a condo, how many rooms?"

A blank stare was all she could offer him. She really hadn't thought this through.

Darby laughed. "This is how most people start out unless they have bought before. The most important thing is to find what you can't live without, and we narrow it down."

The more she thought about it the less certain Jordan was that she wanted to take this on as long as the investigation was still going on. Then again, there'd be another after that. She might never leave. The thought was depressing.

"I don't need that much. I want it to be private, not too far from the city, and move-in ready. I don't have a lot of time—" She laughed wryly. "Or patience for renovations."

"That's a start," he ascertained. "Are there any deadlines you need to observe? How soon would you like to move?"

Yesterday? The truth was, she dreaded this move as much as she anticipated it. This conversation was making it real.

"Soon. I guess. It's a bit...complicated at the moment. I don't have a deadline though. I thought you might be able to show me a few properties. Doesn't have to be super modern, just functional."

"Sure, we can work with that." He handed her a business card. "Why don't you let me take your information, and if you can think of anything else, email me? I'll call you for an appointment."

"Sounds good. Thank you."

"Have a good night, Detective. I hope you're off the clock now?" She hoped he wouldn't waste that charming smile on her for anything other than trying to lay the ground for securing a sale.

"I am." Not counting the hours she'd lie awake going over every single aspect of the workday, of course. "Thanks for seeing me."

Back in her car a few minutes later, Jordan considered her options. She could go home and pretend nothing had changed. After this day, she didn't think Ellie would even still expect her. She also didn't feel like getting scolded again, for professional and other reasons. What did she have to lose? She was halfway out the door already anyway.

Ellie had most definitely expected her. A bluesy tune was playing in the background. Ellie opened the door to her in a short satin robe, under which she was naked. They were past the point of pretending this was anything they were willing to stop. At least, here, nobody could walk in on them, Jordan thought as she sank back against the door, feeling the day's fatigue leaving her body rapidly. Thank God Ellie felt much forgiving about Bethany's untimely appearance, or about any other way Jordan had screwed up in the past days. Her judgment might be clouded by helpless desire, but she couldn't remember the last time she'd felt this appreciated.

"A good evening to you. You've been looking forward to seeing me?" Ellie whispered. It was hard to deny that to a woman who had her hand down your pants, her question already answered.

"All day, since you kind of left me hanging this morning."

"Well, yeah, your girlfriend showing up did not help with the plan."

"Please, don't." To her relief, Ellie didn't mind ending the subject, nor providing another kind of relief right here in the doorway. "You feel so good."

"I hope so. I'm happy to please."

Even as her body strained into the touch, poised for release, Jordan wondered about the women who had asked nothing more, pleasure, a life of their choice, and ended up in the cross-fire of somebody's prejudice and deadly misogyny. For a few heartbeats, all thoughts vanished as she gave in to her climax, simply staying upright requiring all of her concentration. Ellie pulled her close, and Jordan reveled in the brief illusion of being in that warm, safe space with her. Reality would hit soon enough.

"Actually, I don't have beer," Ellie said. "Would you like a glass of wine, before—" She broke off, obviously unsure about what to say. Jordan was already low on morals these days, but she wasn't going to leave without repaying the favor at least. She didn't want to leave at all, if she was honest.

"That would be great." She studied the floor for a moment and then forced herself to hold Ellie's gaze. "Can I stay?"

"Tonight?" Ellie's eyes widened. "You're not going to call her? Forget about it, that's none of my business. I'm not sure I understand what's going on, but yes, of course you can stay. You don't have to convince me."

It was on the tip of her tongue to tell her about the meeting with Darby, but Jordan restrained herself at the last moment. She didn't want to get anyone's hopes up too high, hers or Ellie's.

"Thank you." She wondered if Ellie expected any kind of reassurance, and if she was able to give her any.

Ellie smiled gently. "I assume you'll make it up to me, right? There's something else. Since I haven't been able to go grocery shopping, you may buy me breakfast as well."

She was letting her off easily.

❦

Her arms wrapped around Ellie, Jordan was close to drifting off to sleep. Unlike moments ago, the room was quiet, the peaceful atmosphere misleading. A few hours from now, they'd be back at work, and she'd be facing Bethany. She would have to drop by home to change clothes. The conversation, either at home or at the department, wouldn't be pleasant. She hoped Darby would call her back sooner than later. Once she'd figured out her own life, she might have an idea about how Ellie fit into it, or if she even wanted to.

Ironic how sex with her lover of nine years could make her feel troubled and restless, while for this moment, all the build up tension was gone from her body, leaving her at ease. She'd enjoy the feeling as long as she could.

He logged into the chat room, not surprised at finding a panicky private message. *"They know about Seattle! What are we gonna do?!"*

He snickered. "I'm not sure what you're going to do, buddy, but it sounds like you're in trouble," he said out loud. He had no intention whatsoever of engaging any more with this amateur. Let the police deal with him, which, as it seemed, they were already doing. It could never harm diverting attention for a bit.

Meanwhile, he'd have to figure out what to do about Judy. She wasn't learning as well as he had hoped, defying him at every step. He couldn't afford to have another body turn up, but he wasn't going to bury her in his backyard either.

He sighed to himself. Maybe it was time to intensify the lesson. Maybe she'd get it after all and become the first success story... Judy had been around longer than Lori, and still, she showed no signs of listening to him. His attention was straying. There were too many loose ends, too many stories in need of a better ending. He had been fantasizing about the one that got away, but there were risks to consider. He'd been so certain that night, the woman's outfit and confident gait, click-click-click on the pavement telling him without a doubt that she was in need of a lesson. She still was, no doubt about it, but his priorities were shifting. Some things were meant to be, if risky. He decided not to see Judy tonight, but instead indulge himself with the idea of what he might do a couple of weeks from now.

This one might actually want to be saved.

Pain. Pleasure. He swirled his whiskey on the rocks before he took a deep sip from the tumbler. He was still learning, after all, and nobody was perfect, but he was getting damn close.

Chapter Six

For once, Ellie's sleepless night was not due to nightmares, on the contrary. She was feeling irrationally victorious with the outcome of the day. Not only had Jordan stayed with her, but she hadn't needed any convincing at all, instead she had asked. Ellie's initial shock of being confronted with Bethany at work of all places had made room for curiosity, and, she had to admit, sympathy. Why would Jordan let Bethany treat her this way? Of course, between the FBI and the department, a certain amount of posturing was to be expected, but that wasn't all there was to the story.

The workday brought some movement into their case as well. The autopsy results for Chantal Perron suggested that she'd been subjected to the same drugs as Lori Gleason and Eleanor Campbell.

Ellie was, for the most part of the day, relegated to desk and phone. Apparently, Jordan had no problem defying the sergeant when it came to assignments but felt the need to be more careful with Bethany around. Unnecessary, Ellie thought. So far, they had managed not to ravish each other in an interrogation room. What could go wrong?

The 911 call came in minutes after a lunch break in which most co-workers kept a terse silence, only Bethany seemed to be relaxed and in a good mood. Jordan hardly acknowledged her or Ellie.

The call jolted everyone into action.

"What are you doing?" Jordan asked her partner, irritated, when Bethany shrugged into a Kevlar. "You're not coming."

"Whoa." Bethany kept a polite smile, never raised her voice. "Now's not the time to have that talk about jurisdiction with the sergeant—or my boss. It is out of courtesy that we haven't taken the case away from your division yet."

"Are you even listening to yourself?" Jordan winced when she realized Ellie had been standing close enough to overhear their conversation.

"Do you want me to come?" Ellie asked, trying to sound confident and not as freaked out as she was, by the potential confrontation with the murderer, and the profiler's demeanor. Bethany looked her over before she shook her head. "No thanks, Harding. This is for the big girls."

"Excuse me?"

"You heard me. We don't have time for this."

Henderson gave her a sympathetic shrug.

Ellie was dismissed.

⁂

Several squad cars had already arrived at the scene, barricades erected outside the All Colors. Gleason was becoming unraveled, Jordan thought as she listened to the ramblings of a man who had pretended to be in Spain on business, when in fact, he had met Chantal Perron, a woman who was now dead, in Seattle. He was holding Sheila, the All Colors' bartender, hostage in her workplace. The fact that he had picked up the phone made her carefully optimistic that the situation could be resolved without any more deaths.

"We can talk about this, okay? Just let her go. You'll be in a much better position if you let her go," she told him. She could hear crying in the background. Jordan hoped he hadn't hurt her. If they ended this today, there was still a chance they could find Judy Lawrence alive.

"No! You're just trying to trick me," he accused.

She could feel Bethany rolling her eyes behind her.

"I swear no one's trying to trick you. We want to make sure Sheila is safe. Mr. Gleason, I have some questions for you, but we really don't need her for that. How about I come in, and we talk? Help me understand. We'll leave her out of it."

Bethany drew a sharp breath. "Have you lost your mind? Sergeant Bristol, this is not what we agreed on."

"Okay," Gleason said after a long pause. "You can come in."

"All right. We do this nice and easy. When you open the door to me, you let Sheila go at the same time. Do we have a deal?"

"Leave the gun outside. If you bring a gun inside, I shoot her," he threatened. The woman trapped inside the house whimpered.

"Jordan, for Christ's sake!"

"No, it's okay, I hear you. No gun. We talk."

"This is crazy." Bethany shook her head in an angry, frustrated gesture. "If this is how you do things around here, I'm not surprised at your lack in efficiency."

"Sergeant, we want him alive and talking," Jordan said. "We don't even know if he's the murderer."

Bethany scoffed.

"In any case, we have a chance at talking him down before he hurts her, and if he's our man, we might find Judy Lawrence."

"We might have a chance at getting you killed as well."

"Roberts, that's enough. This is Detective Carpenter's call."

Bethany's lips formed a thin line.

Jordan secretly felt exhilarated, allowing herself a brief moment to acknowledge the emotion. Not only had Bristol backed her up, but Bethany had no way of denying she was right. There was no time to discuss this any longer. While she had a good chance of ending up hurt, Jordan knew she could make a difference today. She knew her job, and her limits. Every once in a while, she had to prove it to Bethany, and herself.

"Mr. Gleason? I'm coming in now."

Crime and punishment. Was it more important to teach the cheater, or the person that dared to come between two partners in a relationship? There was so much work for him to do, but it was tough. Most people weren't cut out for those realities. He turned off the radio, his anger growing by the minute.

The woman stared back at him with wide frightened eyes, dreading the punishment she'd receive. What? He wanted to ask. Is it my fault now that you're a lying, cheating whore?

He went to work.

Ellie couldn't concentrate, a multitude of mixed emotions, none of them good, keeping her mind hostage. Dr. Roberts' unveiled disdain for her was the least of it. Ellie was baffled—how could she know? It wasn't her biggest problem at the moment. She hated to be this far from the action, not knowing what was going on. What she had understood so far was that Bethany and Jordan were in a constant competition, an aspect of their relationship that had seeped into their professional lives long before Ellie was in the picture. Was she, really? What would happen after today?

She was worried about Jordan too. Worried sick. If she'd been on the scene now, doing her job, she wouldn't even have so much time to think about it. Ellie hated being afraid.

She hated that Bethany had told her to stay behind, treating her like a schoolgirl when other uniformed officers had been called in to provide backup.

Jordan had said she was planning on moving out. That gave her a little hope, even though it was no indication they might have a chance.

Please, be okay.

She went over the files again, Gleason, Hayes, Campbell, and now Judy Lawrence. He was wearing a mask the whole time, she remembered Lori Gleason saying. She would have recognized her ex-husband's voice, wouldn't she? Then again, the drugs in her system had to mess with her perception.

"Stop struggling!"

Had it been Gleason who attacked her that night? Would all the strings come together today?

⁂

"What's the point? You won't believe me anyway," he said bitterly, raising the gun once more.

"That's not true." Jordan kept her hands up, fairly proud they weren't shaking. At least, Sheila was outside now. "What's this thing with the collar? I told you, I want to understand."

"It wasn't me. In Seattle, it wasn't me."

"Okay. What happened?"

"They made fun of me. I wanted them to stop," he said, his expression haunted. "It had to stop."

Here we go.

"Them...You mean Lori...and Isabel?"

"I'm not stupid!" he yelled at her. "It was supposed to be a prank. No one was ever supposed to die."

Jordan stood still, unflinching. She would let him talk until something came up that made sense, not let him know that she didn't understand a thing at this moment. It was clear though that Mr. Gleason had a strange idea of a prank. Three women had died, another one was still in danger.

"I believe you. Pranks can get out of hand, turn out in a way you didn't intend."

"Lori was sleeping around, making me look like an idiot. Do you do that to your husband too? Do you expect him to just take it?"

She hadn't seen the blow coming, the butt of the gun connecting painfully with the side of her face before he trained the weapon on her again. It made her stagger back, struggling to keep her balance. She tasted blood.

"No. That's not a good idea. So, you wanted to punish her, make her stop. Is that why you locked her up?"

"I didn't lock her up, stupid!"

"Calm...down, okay? We don't want the cops outside to think this is getting out of hand, right? Tell me about the prank. You went to Seattle. You met Chantal. Was it for payback, to let Lori know you could do the same?"

He was nervous, his finger trembling on the trigger. It might be time to put an end to this situation, and soon.

"He said he'd scare her a little, and I could enjoy myself in the meantime, with Chantal."

"Who said that?"

"It's over," he said darkly. "You won't believe me anyway. It's only a matter of time before you connect the dots, and I won't go to prison." This time, he raised the gun to his own head. Jordan acted without thinking, trying to get hold of his wrist.

A shot rang out, and then another. If he died, they might never find Lawrence.

Gleason dropped to the floor, screaming in pain, the side of his head bloody, but he hadn't managed to put a bullet in his brain. Kicking the gun out of his reach, Jordan stepped back, catching her breath. "I'm sorry, Mr. Gleason. You'll have to answer some more questions about who put you up to this."

She felt her knees go weak and reached for the table behind her to steady herself.

Chapter Seven

No one had died, which was a relief, but there was still a lot of work left to do. Back at the station, Jordan went to clean herself up in the bathroom. She looked a bit worse for wear, but with the blood cleaned away, it wasn't so bad. She returned to her desk hoping to sit down for a few minutes and clear her head. As expected, the moment of peace didn't last long.

"You should go to the hospital." Bethany's tone sounded more chiding than worried, but maybe that was Jordan's imagination. Ellie hovered close as well, looking scared. Jordan thought it might be as much for her as her looks had to be triggering to someone who had been beaten up not so long ago.

"I'm fine," Jordan said, pressing the ice pack against her face, wishing she could block out all the concerned people around her. Gleason had lost consciousness and was in the hospital, ironically the same from which Lori was about to be released. There was nothing for her to do there.

They had to talk to Sheila and take apart Gleason's apartment for any hint of something that could support his ramblings.

Punishment. Bethany had been right. Of course she had been.

"We have the warrant for Gleason?" Jordan asked, receiving a nod from Henderson. "Fine. You can go ahead," she told him.

"Take Harding and McCarthy. I'll join you right after I talk to Sheila." The bartender was waiting in an interview room, shaken but ready and willing to answer questions after she'd been provided with hot coffee and a snack. "All right. Anything else?"

"I'll wait for you," Bethany said. "You can't drive like this."

"I'd prefer you go over to Gleason's and do your thing." The truth was, Bethany was incredibly gifted in her field, and intuitive. She'd find proof of Gleason's delusions, whatever they meant in detail. Jordan wasn't yet sure if the second man existed at all. Bethany agreed with her on that, surprisingly.

"A few minutes won't change anything," she argued anyway. "Don't be so stubborn."

"I do believe that time is of importance here." Bethany frowned at Bristol's statement. "Why don't you join the officers at Gleason's house, and Officer Harding can drive Detective Carpenter when she's done here?"

Jordan gave him a tired smile. "That's a brilliant idea."

<hr />

"Oh God, I was so scared," Sheila whispered. "I thought he was trying to kill me."

Welcome to the club, Jordan thought wryly, but she kept her musings to herself. Ellie, standing in the corner of the room, looked freaked out enough already.

"Well, it's a good thing you called 911," Jordan acknowledged. "You've been checked out, everything's okay?"

Sheila nodded, biting her lip.

"Is he...You know? Did he kill anybody?"

"We don't know for sure yet. Did he tell you anything? How did you know him in the first place?"

The woman wrapped her hands around the paper cup as if trying to draw warmth from it.

"The women were all kidnapped and drugged before they were murdered, right? I read about that."

Jordan sat up straighter, wincing. It wasn't such a bad idea to have a designated driver. Hopefully there would be some hint at Gleason's apartment as to what happened to Judy Lawrence. She couldn't possibly make it an early night as long as they still didn't have any idea where she was, headache or not. "We believe so."

"I swear I didn't know," Sheila said, the despair in her voice startling. It wasn't surprising considering a man had held a gun to her head earlier today, but Jordan suspected there was another reason. "He owed me money, that's why he came over today. At least I thought it was why, but I think he wanted to make sure there'd be no witness."

"A witness to what?"

"If this helps you to solve the murders, you won't charge me, will you?" She sounded hopeful now.

"Depending on what it is you're going to tell me, we'll certainly take that into consideration," Jordan promised.

Sheila gave a heartfelt sigh, her grip tightening on the cup. "All right. At first, I didn't make the connection at all, but then I saw his photo in the newspaper, and...I swear, I didn't know he was Lori's husband. He was hanging out at the All Colors on nights Lori wasn't there, watching. Someone had given him a tip, I don't know who. He bought some stuff..."

"Stuff?"

"Well, all kinds, to get high. Not the usual. Somebody told him he could get it from me, but the bastard never paid me. Then I put two and two together. He didn't want to get high, he wanted to use them on someone he kept locked up in the basement."

"When did you make that connection?"

"He was babbling crazy, about Seattle and the policewoman who got attacked, swore he didn't do it, that someone was trying to frame him."

"What did he say about the policewoman?"

Sheila shrugged. "Not much, just that it wasn't him, and she wasn't even his type. I couldn't make sense of any of that, I was scared, you know?"

Gleason had known about the attack on Ellie. If he had told the truth, the perpetrator was still out there, and whether he was playing a game of numbers or not, he was likely the same man who had kidnapped Judy and Lori and murdered the others.

Jordan dared to turn and look at Ellie. She had gone pale.

"He's been lying to us from the start," Ellie said when they were on their way to Gleason's house. "I can see him going off the deep end over all of this. Maybe he started out wanting to punish his wife, but then got into the killing. Whatever. He's in the hospital now, so he can hardly harm me or anyone else."

Jordan let her ramble on before she undid Ellie's argument. "Eleanor Campbell was killed long before Lori disappeared, and besides the M.O., there's no connection between the two."

Ellie groaned. "I'm so tired of this. Even Dr. Roberts thinks he's the one, and isn't she supposed to be the expert?" Not a good idea, she reflected, bringing up the third party between them. Jordan looked unhappy, her shoulders tense.

"I've been on this case since we found the first body. She hangs out with the PD in Seattle, learns some facts, and doesn't even tell me? I hate this *bureau*-cratic shit."

If the situation hadn't been this serious, Ellie might have congratulated her on the pun. As it was, she was trying hard not to overreact to what they had learned from Sheila.

"Either way, it's shitty of a husband to get someone to kidnap and torture his wife," she offered. "Even if they were—" She stopped herself short of saying "cheating." Ellie didn't think the reminder would be welcome. Speaking of which. "Can you come over tonight? You've had a rough day. I could cook you something."

It wasn't likely, but she had to try. First of all, once reality sank in that her attacker might have been a serial murderer on the prowl for his next victim, she'd freak. In that case, Ellie would rather be with someone. Second, the sex they had made her feel amazing. She wasn't ready to give up on it yet. Certainly not for the sake of Bethany who was scornful and patronizing even after Jordan had survived a confrontation with an armed and dangerous man.

"I don't know," Jordan said. At least she was honest.

How can you stand her? Ellie wanted to ask. She held back the question, knowing her judgment was clouded by hormones, fear and something that was too early to determine. She was well aware she was walking a fine line. Her new no holds barred approach to life wasn't supposed to come with heartbreak. "I understand you said you wanted to move out, but how are you still together?" It wasn't diplomatic enough.

"You're right, it's been a rough day. I'd like to get this done and head home. There'll be an officer in front of your house. If there ever was another guy, and I think it's a possibility, he might be tempted to make an appearance."

Ellie leaned back in her seat, trying to get a handle on her disappointment.

"We don't know if he ever planned to come back for me."

"That's right. I don't want to take that chance."

"I'd feel safer though if you were with me," she hazarded.

Jordan shook her head. "No way. We've crossed enough lines. Your safety is no joke."

"Oh, so that other thing is a joke? I feel so much better now."

"Ellie."

"You're right. We're at work. This is not the right time to discuss these things." She avoided Jordan's gaze, startled when, at the next red light, Jordan laid her hand over Ellie's.

"Either way, I'll clean up this mess," she promised.

Ellie didn't know what to say.

⁂

They found the rope in the garage, a worn leather collar in the bedroom, none of it a surprise anymore. When Ellie stumbled over the threshold between the dining and the living room, she wondered if it was mere fatigue, but then she realized there was an irregularity in the floor. It was too small to be another trap door, but when she tried, the wooden plank came off after a couple of attempts.

"Detective!"

Jordan was beside her in an instant, her jaw dropping slightly at the sight of the papers in the hiding place. Neat, hand drawn maps. Floor plans. They had always been certain that the victims hadn't been chosen at random but based on habits and lifestyles the perpetrator perceived as a crime. According to these sketches, neither had been the places where they'd been held. A quick check revealed there were more than the names they had. The bastard had been planning ahead.

"Good job," she said, about to continue when her cell phone rang. "Check each location, and then make sure these are bagged and off to Evidence." There was a hint of excitement to her voice, and Ellie knew why. They could find the place where

Judy Lawrence was held today. "Oh hey," she said to the caller. "Could you call later? I'm at work. Really? That's great. Hang on a minute." Jordan walked away a few steps, making Ellie curious about who might have interrupted with the good news. The truth was, she knew next to nothing about the woman whose body she knew intimately, family, friends, anything. Maybe Jordan would tell her. She didn't hold her breath.

She had a job to do. Kate and Jensen joined her, and they began bagging the papers and marking down the information each of them held.

The house they hadn't been able to match with a victim's name yet was empty, but lived in. The family of four was on a one-month vacation according to their neighbors, lovely people who had moved in not long ago. The elderly lady next door seemed happy and excited to talk to the police. Maybe, Jordan thought, she was just lonely, grateful for any kind of human interaction. She wondered if she was going to end up the same. For sure, she didn't seem all that successful at making a relationship work. Ellie might be attracted to her now, but she hadn't yet experienced the everyday life with Jordan. Ask Bethany about it. On second thought, don't.

Despite the reassurances she had given everyone, Jordan felt exhausted, the pounding headache not helping her overall condition. She didn't want to go home and sit on the couch when this could be their chance to find Judy.

She felt a drop of sweat snake down her spine when they eased down the narrow stairs to the unfinished basement. It was cold and drafty down here, obvious that the owners hadn't invested much in this part of the house.

The basement was empty. She felt lightheaded and sick with disappointment. Maybe she should take Ellie's offer after all, but she had already committed to another appointment. Ellie was right, actually. There was no reason for her to keep stalling any longer. Once she closed on a new place, Bethany would realize she was serious and let her go. Jordan wasn't yet sure whether she was thrilled or terrified at the prospect. There wasn't anything particularly devilish about Bethany, but without a doubt, she was the one Jordan knew.

She knew Jordan better than anyone else. Sometimes, trusting too much was dangerous, giving the other person too much power over you.

A quick search revealed nothing but what appeared to be links from a golden necklace or bracelet. It was something. It had to be.

***

"Ouch." Darby winced at the sight of her. "Bad day, I assume?"

Jordan shrugged. "It could have been worse."

"Wow. I don't think I'd be able to do your job, and frankly I'm grateful I don't have to. However, I think I have something to take your mind off it. Let's go take a look."

They had met in a neighborhood about half an hour away from the city center. It wasn't exactly close to work, but distance in every way appealed to Jordan.

"The owner is looking to make a quick sale, because she's leaving the country due to a new job," the realtor explained. "It's not big but updated and move-in ready."

"Sounds good to me."

They walked up the steps to the small porch, and he unlocked the door for her. Jordan stepped inside and felt like she could finally breathe. The prospect of having this space, any space, to herself put a smile on her face she hadn't been aware of until the realtor mentioned it.

"You like it."

"What's not to like?" Jordan ran her hand over the countertop. The kitchen opened up into a dining space with a huge window, letting in lots of light. As Darby had said, the rooms were medium-sized, but it would be more than enough for her. She hadn't lived by herself in almost a decade, and the thought excited her. "This is enough space. I love the fact that I could just pack a few things and move in here."

"If you like the furniture, you could negotiate with the owner. She's not going to bring it to Japan. You must have something you'd want to bring though?"

"Not that much. I paid half, but my partner chose most of it." She laughed wryly. "That sounds bad. Truth is, I'm not good at shopping for anything, so whenever I don't have to, that's a definite plus."

"You broke up?" he asked, his tone sympathetic, before he caught himself. "I'm sorry. I didn't mean to be nosy. It's often the case when someone comes looking for a new place by themselves."

"I guess you hear a lot of stories. Well, you're not too far off in this case."

"Then I'm even more sorry," he said. "Why don't we take a look at the bedroom?"

"I'd like that."

Off the master bedroom, there was a small balcony, and a deck below, the property encased by a cedar hedge. The half-hour drive every morning was something to consider, but truth be told, this house already felt like a home. It could be hers.

The master bedroom was the biggest room in the house, with an adjacent bathroom, everything modern and functional, but not daunting like the perfect magazine home Bethany aspired to have. A smaller room for office space, another half bath.

"I love it," Jordan said. "How soon can I move in?"

"Whoa." Without a doubt, Jonathan Darby was pleased. "I haven't even told you that it's a five-minute walk to the water. I'm glad you like it. Frankly, it's a steal, which brings me to the next subject."

"Anything under three-fifty, I'm ready to make an offer."

"Usually, I'm the one who has to help speed things up a bit. In this case, I think it's good to make up your mind quickly, because the owner is on a tight timetable. I want you to be sure though. We should see a couple more places, just to show you what options are out there, maybe even something closer to town. If you still like this one best, I'll prepare an offer for you."

A few years back, she and Bethany had thought about home ownership, and Jordan was now glad they had decided to rent. However, she had gotten an idea of what kind of money the bank would let her spend. "How about I'll check with my bank, and I meet you tomorrow to sign the papers?"

"Do you always make up your mind so quickly, Detective?"

Yes, and it gets me in trouble every single time, she thought, even before he reached out to touch her arm, letting the touch linger, longer than it was appropriate for their kind of relationship. She should have discouraged him there and then, as she was in enough trouble already. It had always been hard for Jordan to resist playing with fire, even after getting burned a few times. A harmless flirt didn't harm anyone. The realtor didn't seem like the type who'd involve her in yet another tug of war of emotions. He was a guy, after all. There was no danger.

"Hello stranger," Bethany greeted her when she entered the apartment. She seemed in a good mood. She'd better be when Jordan disclosed her plans of moving out. Surveying the apartment, Jordan realized she hadn't exaggerated. She could pack and be out of here in a couple of hours. Maybe she had never really moved in.

"I'm sorry I'm late," she said.

"Didn't you see my message? I was worried about you. Anyway, have a seat. I ordered dinner, it should be here any moment. I've got good news too. I lit a fire under the lab and made them work overtime, and guess whose DNA was on that piece of bracelet?"

"You tell me."

"You're no fun," Bethany chided, but her tone was affectionate. "It's Lori Gleason's, and guess what, she said she wasn't wearing it on the day she was taken. Once Gleason is ready to be questioned, we'll figure it all out. Your rookie had good instincts."

"Yeah. Anything else?" Jordan preferred not to deepen the subject of Ellie. It would only make her regret she couldn't be with her now.

"Well, given the fact a crazy person hit you in the face today, I can understand you're grumpy. Sit. Some wine and food will make you feel better. I'm sure you couldn't even tell me when's the last time you ate. Anyway. I believe he's taking trophies, either before he's kidnapping them, or he's bold enough to return to their home after he took them. Not that it would be so unusual for a serial murderer, but it gives us something else to look out for. See if Judy's sister can tell something is missing, and who had access to it."

"That's good." Jordan had checked the papers found under the plank herself before she went to meet Darby. Every place that didn't match a victim had been examined, and they had found nothing. With each minute ticking by, Judy Lawrence's fate looked worse. She was tired. What if they, if she was overlooking something? A change of a place to live might not be all she should consider.

"Don't tear yourself up over it," Bethany said softly. "You're a good cop. You can't win them all."

"It's not a game. People's lives are at stake."

The doorbell rang before Bethany could answer. "Hold that thought," she said.

He took a fleeting look at his mirror image in the window, smiling. The look suited him. His mother had always said he should become a doctor. He didn't really have the talent. It had taken him forever to make the drugs work in his favor, have his subjects relaxed but not comatose, distracted but not in a full-blown psychotic break.

He was still learning.

He kept his head down as he walked along the hallway, to the room he was looking for.

He had weighed his chances, thought about mistakes made along the way. He had to be careful. Of course, there would come a moment when he wouldn't want to share the glory any longer, when the world would know, but he had so much to accomplish before that.

He had so much knowledge to give to the world. Reassured in that thought, he went about his work quietly, then left. He walked out unseen, onto the parking lot and to the car he had rented today.

Another loose end tied up.

He laughed softly to himself. Tied up. He couldn't wait to start his next project, though he would have to be patient a little while longer, see if Judy could make any progress at all.

He thought about the cop, and her inevitable lesson, within a few heartbeats breathless with arousal. He smiled at his image in the rearview mirror. *Patience, my friend. You always finish what you start, even with her.*

Chapter Eight

A s Ellie hung up the phone, Kate appeared in front of the desk she temporarily occupied. "Hey, Ellie," she said. "We hardly ever see you anymore. I know you're playing with the big kids these days, but please, join us for just one drink tonight, okay? Everyone needs a little break."

Ellie shrugged. "Sure. Why not?" She wasn't kidding herself. If Jordan had given her any indication she'd invite herself to Ellie's home and bed tonight, a drink with friends would have been the last thing on her mind. It was unlikely to happen.

She'd had another bad night. On top of that, she had the suspicion she and Jensen would be sent back to their regular day job soon. From there it would be many more months until she could take the detective's exam. Meanwhile Jordan and Bethany seemed to have patched things up, or maybe that was just their usual pattern.

Either way, it probably meant Ellie was on her way out. She shouldn't feel so dejected about it—life hadn't paid her back enough yet for bleeding on the sidewalk at the hands of a sexist, probably murdering, jerk. Due to him, she now needed a security detail, an officer in an unmarked car on the street that made her feel claustrophobic in her own home. No, she wasn't done collecting. The problem was, she didn't want just any warm body next to her in her bed. She wanted Jordan.

"That is awesome. By the way, I'm a little jealous of you, you know?" Kate said. "Working with a real FBI profiler, that is so cool. Does she go around and see scenes of the killing happen?"

"Oh my God, you watch too much TV. She's a psychiatrist," Ellie grumbled, and Kate laughed.

"You got up on the wrong side of the bed today. I better leave you to it now. I'll see you later."

"Yes, you will." Ellie tried not to stare at the scene a few feet away, Jordan and Bethany conferring about something that was no doubt case related. Despite the problems that were obvious to the attentive listener, they did have a certain connection in their professional lives that would take Ellie years to reach if she ever got there. It wasn't fair.

Interrupting them felt like talking to seniors on her first day in junior high. She had to do it though. Reluctantly, she got up walked over to where Jordan and Bethany were standing, immersed in their conversation.

"Um, excuse me?" Ellie began.

She could only describe the look Bethany gave her as someone patient with a person who wasn't quite up to their standards. Maybe she was imagining things. Too little sleep could make that happen. "Meg Lawrence called. Judy Lawrence's sister? She's on her way here."

Jordan and Bethany exchanged a meaningful look. Ellie found it unnerving.

"She said something was missing from Judy's room, some coins. Apparently, Judy was a collector. Anyway, she's going to tell you."

"Thank you, Ellie," Jordan said, giving her a warm smile that was a stark contrast to Bethany's expression. Ellie wished she could tempt her one more time. Maybe tonight.

Meg Lawrence had the distracted look of someone who hadn't slept in days. "I'm so sorry. I can't believe I didn't notice this earlier."

"It's okay," Jordan assured her. "This is a difficult time for you."

"It sure is. I'm not even sure how much I can help you. Judy has been collecting those old coins for years, but I only realized there were some missing because of the empty spaces. Medieval, I think? Maybe you can find that stuff on the Internet."

Jordan looked at Bethany. Her theory about the killer taking trophies might be valid, but neither of them had any expertise when it came to this particular field. "Do you know how much the collection or parts of it are worth?" If there was money to be made, the perpetrator might reconsider keeping them.

Meg shrugged. "I always thought that was a nerdy hobby. Judy wasn't—" She swallowed hard. "Isn't rich by any means unless she was hiding something from me. I mean, she moved in with me to save money." Meg studied her hands on the table. "Now I wished I hadn't been nagging all the time. She probably needed a timeout after the divorce, and I've been giving her a hard time. Now I might never see her again!" She started crying.

Jordan felt inadequate because she had hardly anything to console her. There was a possibility that she might never be able to make up with her sister. They'd have to check another ex-husband's alibi.

"When did she get divorced?" she asked. "Judy went back to her maiden name?"

"She never gave it up in the first place," Meg said. "The marriage didn't last long, not even two years. Not that the name has anything to do with it. I guess they weren't compatible. They got drunk and married in Vegas, should have been their first clue. They finalized the divorce last summer."

"Could you give us a name and address?"

Meg Lawrence's eyes widened. "You don't think he could have anything to do with it?"

"We'd like to rule that out," Jordan told her and held out a legal pad and pen to her. Obediently, Meg jotted down the information and handed the pad back to Jordan.

"Thanks." She excused herself to step aside and pass the information on to Derek. When she came back, she saw Bethany reached out to touch the distraught woman's arm.

"We'll find her," she said softly.

Jordan remembered when she had scolded Ellie for making promises. This was different though. Bethany hadn't promised they'd find Judy alive, her omission gone unnoticed by the sister. The phone on her desk rang, and she excused herself. A moment later, she barely suppressed a curse.

"Ellie!"

Ellie stood in front of her a heartbeat later. "You talked to Ms. Lawrence earlier? I'd like you to drive her home, see if you can find anything on that coin collection, where she bought them from, where someone might be able to sell them. When you come back, leave everything here with me or Derek. He's going to check on the ex, but I assume he'll be here soon."

"Where will you be?" Ellie asked.

"Something came up," she said curtly. "We talk when I'm back here. Ms. Lawrence, thanks for coming in. Officer Harding will take it from here."

When they were out of earshot, Bethany cast her a curious look. "Okay, enlighten me."

Jordan groaned. "I wish there was anything enlightening about this case. Gleason died in the hospital, cause unknown."

"Damn." Bethany made a face. "Bullet got him?"

"I don't know. I don't think so. The doctor was hopeful that he would wake up."

"If another body turns up, we know he told the truth about the second man," she mused.

"I'd rather wrap this up before another body turns up," Jordan said, picking up her keys. Bethany's gaze was almost pitying.

<hr/>

"I'm sorry we can't tell you more," the doctor said, her look apologetic. "Of course, there can be complications with gunshot wounds, but this is sudden. I guess the autopsy will tell you more. So far, we can't detect anything out of place."

If this guy was unorganized, changing plans at last moment's notice, why did he keep slipping through their fingers? Was it possible that Gleason had made the whole story about a second perpetrator up? She hated doubting herself.

"You were tossing and turning all night," Bethany said when they left the hospital room. "Let me buy you a coffee. We can keep discussing the case if that makes you feel any better."

"No need to be sarcastic," Jordan muttered. "I'll take the coffee though."

Bethany, as usual, was well organized. She had copies of the map and index cards with her. That intuitive profiler thing Ellie thought she was doing? Jordan knew that Bethany's skills flourished more within her slightly OCD personality, categories, patterns, shaking up the pieces until you found the one that fit. Once upon a time, they had worked well together.

"Lori Gleason is alive," Bethany reminded her, heading straight for the coffee shop across the street from the hospital. "You can't always win."

"If there is a second man, he'll continue the killing, every woman he thinks overstepped the boundaries he set."

"That's a depressing thought," Bethany acknowledged. "Two Vanilla Lattes," she told the barista, and they found a place by the window farthest from the student typing away on his laptop, and the couple of doctors off their shift.

"So. How serious are you about this girl?"

"I don't want to talk about it," Jordan said, before she even could acknowledge how inappropriate and awkward the subject was here and now. Sooner or later, she knew she would have to answer this question, but this was not the moment.

Bethany got up to get their beverages. "I think I deserve to know," she said when she sat back down. "If you needed to get her out of your system, that's one thing. If it's worse than that, I need to know what to prepare myself for."

"Come on." Would anyone really be surprised that she was buying a place for herself, out of the city? "She's had a rough time."

"Well, yeah, someone had to console her, I guess. I hear she wants to be a detective."

"Bethany, stop it."

"She's young, pretty, flexible, I guess, but don't fool yourself. When this is all over, you'll need someone to pick up the pieces. You know how it goes."

"You might be surprised." Jordan took a sip of her coffee, torn between annoyance about Bethany choosing her drink without asking, and the small comfort it presented. She thought of the fireplace in the house she'd seen. Home. All hers.

"You know I'll always be that person, right? I'll always be there for you. I promised. Now, let's talk about the case. Maybe we can come up with anything before we go bother Lori again. Oh, and I'm sorry we have to talk about Ellie. Apparently, she is on someone's radar too. It could have been Gleason. He fits the description she gave."

"What are you saying, that this case is really closed and I haven't caught up to it yet?"

"You have to consider the possibility. You're exhausted. I think you haven't completely recovered from—"

"Can we stay on topic for the next five minutes?" Jordan interrupted her harshly.

Bethany shrugged. "As you wish. Between you and me, I'll say this: All the women were screwing around. Someone took offense to that. Let's say he offered Gleason a solution but wanted to stay in the shadows himself. Gleason is responsible for finding the tools—drugs, rope, a little kinky twist, but the actual killing of people makes him queasy. How did he find this punisher guy?"

"I'm thinking he found Gleason. He chose the targets and then looked at anyone who might have an interest in hurting these women, diverting attention."

Bethany looked doubtful. "These boys don't easily trust others, and he would have to find a new 'partner' with each woman? Maybe he worked that way with Gleason, if 'he' actually exists. When exactly did you start sleeping with her?"

"What?"

"It was after the attack, wasn't it? That is strange. Maybe he boasted to Gleason, but it wasn't him after all. Unless going after women in relationships is Harding's M.O. Do you know anything about it except the obvious?"

The coffee had gone cold, tasting sickly sweet now. "Look, I am...sorry." They both knew something was wrong with this picture. Neither of them would acknowledge it, as usual. "What I know is she didn't deserve to be beaten and nearly worse, and neither did any of the women deserve what was done to them."

"I respect your emotions, even though they are not very helpful at the moment. Let's go see Lori," Bethany said.

"Don't expect me to cry," Lori said before she burst into tears. Jordan had the feeling it wasn't entirely out of grief for her late ex-husband.

"Oh God," she said, "You don't think I had anything to do with it?"

"Why would you? You said you had a good marriage, parted as friends. He told us the same," Bethany said.

It took a while before Lori answered. Jordan thought it made sense she was struggling to find words, because at some point, they did a poor job to reflect an overwhelming reality. Bethany, she knew, felt the opposite. Words, to her, meant clarity and direction. Maybe Jordan was lacking both these days.

"The truth is our marriage wasn't that great. I'm sure he never mentioned it to you, because it was no big deal to him, but he used to belittle me at every turn. I didn't feel free until I went shopping for an apartment of my own."

This is something I can relate to, Jordan thought. Not that she was an abused spouse in any sense of the word, but the idea of having a place of her own meant freedom.

"Isn't that crap?" Lori asked. "Even now, a man can do whatever he wants. If we have different ideas of what we like or need, they look down on us. Like that fucker..." She was choking up. Jordan, who agreed with the sentiment in general, caught Bethany's thoughtful look.

"During the time of your marriage, did you ever cheat?"

"What's that supposed to mean?" Lori asked, unveiled anger in her voice. "I've had it with people saying more or less how I deserved this because my sex life didn't fit their neat and boring little ideas. You're a shrink, right? I might be some sort of deviant in your eyes, but I never hurt anyone. I was strung up in a moldy basement for days. Now I hear the same guy killed Bella. Why can't you just leave me alone?"

"We will," Jordan assured her. "I'm sorry."

She thought of the time she had visited Lori at the hospital, with Ellie. Lori must have read her mind, because she said, in a calmer tone, "Your colleague, how is she doing?"

"She's ok."

"Did you catch that guy, at least?"

"Not yet."

Lori scoffed. "I figured. All right, if there isn't anything else? I'd like to celebrate the fact that at least he is never going to bother me again."

"Just one more question," Bethany said. "Did anybody approach you recently to talk about your ex, or did you tell anyone about how he belittled you?"

Lori shook her head. "I know where you want to go with this, but I have to disappoint you. Unless my eighty-year-old mother came all the way from Texas to get back at him for stealing the best years of my life...I don't know. Look, he was a nuisance, and he never had any respect for me, which is bad enough, but he wasn't my worst nightmare. I believe someone killed him, and I guess you do too, otherwise you wouldn't be here. I can't help you."

"You've helped a lot," Jordan said. "Again, I'm sorry."

Chapter Nine

I n the afternoon meeting, Bristol updated everyone working in and with the unit, and Bethany painted the picture emerging of the perpetrator. Ellie knew she should have listened more closely—after all, this concerned her—but she was distracted. On the bright side, no one had sent her back on the beat yet, but she was aware her days with the task force were counted. Would Bethany eventually go back to work out of headquarters, and would that make any difference for her? Ellie wasn't so sure.

Since she'd spent the night, Jordan had been friendly but distant. With Bethany, she acted compliant, at least what Ellie could see in the workplace. There was an underlying tension between the two, and for the life of her, Ellie couldn't tell what it meant for their relationship in the long run. Were they on the verge of breaking up, or was this the norm for them?

She suppressed a sigh. How had she gotten from taking whatever she could get out of life to trying to figure out Jordan Carpenter? Jordan was thinking about moving out. That sounded like a new start, but it was unclear if that new start could include Ellie in any way.

She missed her. She wasn't going to wait forever either. The next time the opportunity arose, she'd press her for answers. Life was full of surprises, as Ellie had learned the painful way, not all of them good. She wasn't going to waste time hanging on to a lost cause.

A lost cause, this was likely to be.

Ellie had tentatively tried to go back to old habits, changing into a top and short skirt, and a pair of pumps after work. So far so good, or maybe not, because she was sitting with the people who had been her friends since the academy, while Jordan and Bethany had chosen another corner of the bar, a couple of detectives with them.

When Ellie caught Jordan's apologetic gaze, she hoped Jordan was feeling a little sorry at least—for herself. She crossed her legs on the barstool, taking a sip from her glass. She'd take a cab later, no more walking home in the darkness. She liked to tell herself that she didn't change her habits to accommodate a faceless man who had attacked her on the street, but for safety reasons.

She still had an officer in front of her door. Ellie didn't want to make his job harder than necessary. Maybe she should offer Jordan the room previously occupied by Rhonda, her ex-roommate with benefits. That, she figured, would solve most of their problems. Then again, she could tell from the couple's body language that Bethany didn't yet know about Jordan's plans—either that, or she didn't care, and that wasn't the impression Ellie had gotten.

"You are daydreaming again," Kate accused her. "So, what is it like to work an actual serial killer case? You also found the map in Gleason's house. They must be looking forward to having you move upstairs for good next year."

"Yeah, right, they can't wait." Too late, it registered with Ellie that Kate wasn't to blame for any of her current issues, that she was just an interested and supportive friend. "I'm sorry. I hoped we could talk about something else."

"Yeah, sure. Libby here has been dating Wes for almost a month."

"No way!"

Libby laughed. "Now why is that so unbelievable? You've been hanging out with these guys so long already, you've missed a lot."

Ellie knew that Libby had set her sights on an officer from another division, but she didn't have any idea they'd gotten serious. That's what happened when your life stayed on track. "Well, congrats. This is good news at least." Never mind the fact she was feeling slightly jealous about it, and, well, sorry for herself. "Also calls for a new round. I'll pay, since I'm the one who has been neglecting all of you."

"That's what we like to hear," Libby said. "We're so glad to have you back."

"Yeah, because I pay for your booze. I'm kidding! I'm happy for you!" Ellie slid off her barstool and hugged her friend. "I'll be right back."

On her way to the bar, she passed by the detectives' table. It might be coincidence, but Bethany chose that moment to place her hand on Jordan's knee. *I don't like you*, Ellie thought. She admired the woman for her stellar career, and even inebriated, she wouldn't be caught talking trash about her or any other cop, woman. That didn't mean Ellie didn't resent her. The feeling was probably mutual, and if she was honest, she knew Bethany had more of a reason. With resignation, she turned away from the image and gave the bartender her order.

Tonight, it seemed fairly safe to drown her sorrow.

❦

"Hey Judy. We have a visitor tonight. I'll need you to be very quiet." He could swear her eyes were mocking him. Of course, gagged like that, she wouldn't be able to make much of a noise. He guessed by now she had realized this room was pretty much soundproof. Generations of parents who had punished wayward girls down here without anyone hearing them scream. It was the perfect location. Not the perfect subject though.

Her eyes widened, as if she could read something in his gaze, something that told her this guest could mean bad news for her. She was probably right.

He was bored with her already, she wasn't learning well, and there were only so many chances you could give an unwilling and resisting subject. He didn't have time to deal with her tonight though. He walked the length of the room, aware and fascinated by the air being thick with fear. It always happened, sooner or later.

He thought of the cop, struggling underneath him on the unyielding sidewalk, wondering if she was wearing those high heels again. He abandoned the thought abruptly. It was getting late.

⌘

Ellie made a show out of washing her hands at the sink, slowly and methodically, or maybe she was just too drunk to do it any other way. Jordan who stood in the corner, arms crossed over her chest, seemed fairly amused.

There was no one else in the restroom. "You're staring at my hands. Good memories?"

"You should know," Jordan said, her voice a dark and lusty tone.

"Really." Ellie smiled at her reflection in the mirror before she turned around. "What do we do about it? You can't come to my apartment because there's someone guarding my life and virtue. Obviously, I can't come to yours. That's a dilemma."

Jordan didn't say anything, but her expression spoke volumes.

"This is something I've never done before—or wanted to, but I believe this place is fairly sanitary, and my hands are really clean. Let me take care of you?" Ellie asked.

"I can't." If the pained whisper was any indication of how much Jordan wanted to, Ellie had reason to be optimistic.

"Sure you can," she said, taking Jordan's hand and pulling her with her into the stall. Ellie nearly stumbled which might have been because of her stilettos, the alcohol, or an overwhelming desire—or all of the above. Their kiss was deep and messy, with the urgency of two people who had no time to waste. Jordan didn't put up any more resistance. Leaning back against the wall, she closed her eyes, a gasp escaping her lips when Ellie pushed her hand into her slacks and beneath her panties. "You missed me too, right?"

"Oh God. Yes." It might have been an answer to Ellie's question, or appreciation of her actions.

"Shh." Even in her high heels, she had to stretch a bit, her words whispered against Jordan's mouth. "You have to be quiet." She obliged, though the shudder running through her body gave Ellie an idea of how hard it had to be. Staying quiet was hard for Ellie, too, at this point.

"Bossy much, are you?"

"You like that."

Jordan's gaze was clouded with lust. "You seem to be enjoying yourself as well."

"I am," Ellie confirmed. "You feel so good, all hot and..." Then she had to pause and kiss Jordan again to stop her from crying out. The world vanished for a moment in blissful ecstasy before reality and their surroundings registered with them once more.

The sound of Jordan's cell phone ringing made them both jump. "I'm sorry," Jordan said, still breathless. She could mean many things. *Sorry, there's no time to return the favor. Sorry, but this has to be the last time.*

"Take it," Ellie said. "I'll go freshen up."

"Ellie, wait a second—"

"It's okay. When you've figured things out, you know where to find me."

"Yes." Her tone was a lot less polite than Jordan had intended. There was no need to bite the caller's head off because her own life was a mess.

"Detective Carpenter, good evening. I wanted to ask if you can still make it to our appointment."

"Oh." As much as she was looking forward to moving out, Jordan had completely forgotten about the contract she was supposed to sign tonight. When Bethany had sometimes wondered how she got the job done, she hadn't been too far off. Sometimes, Jordan wondered too. "I'm sorry about that...Something came up."

"I figured," he said evenly. "I know I'm the one who advised you to slow it down a bit, but I have to inform you the owner might have another offer on the table. If I can get your signature tonight, the house is yours. Otherwise, you could end up in a bidding war."

"Wow." Jordan heard the faucet being turned off, and a moment later, the sound of the door opening and closing. She tried to focus on the matter at hand. This was quick. Maybe she had conveniently forgotten about the appointment because she wasn't ready to make a decision, but too much had changed since that first night with Ellie. She couldn't pretend everything was fine anymore, to Bethany, to herself. "What do I need to do?"

"Could you meet me at my house?" he asked. "We could finalize the paperwork, and I'll see the owner first thing in the morning. I'm sorry if this is inconvenient, but it seemed to me you really liked the place."

"I did. Okay. Let's do this."

"Good. Let me give you the address, and I'll see you there."

How she was going to explain this to Bethany, Jordan had no idea, but in a way, she was looking forward to that conversation, the opportunity to present to her she had made this consequential adult decision all by herself. She wasn't old enough to settle, out of fear or laziness.

She finally left the stall and went to find Bethany, feeling a bit lightheaded the moment they were face to face. A call to her realtor wasn't all that had happened in the bathroom stall. Jordan could feel her face flush.

"Hey. I need to run a quick errand. I'll see you later at home." She didn't dare look at Ellie who sat with her friends a few feet away. Just the thought of her brought back flashes, making her body tingle with the memory. Jordan wished she could spend the night. Maybe there was a possibility, something, for the two of them once she had the living arrangements figured out. Bethany would go to work at headquarters sooner or later. She'd be fine.

"What errand?" Bethany asked. "If it's about the case, shouldn't I know about it?"

Jordan ignored the reproach. "This case is not the only one I'm working on. You don't have to wait up for me."

"Are you going to see her?" Bethany had no reservations, staring openly and with resentment at Ellie.

"No," Jordan said, before she turned to go.

She sat behind the wheel for a few minutes, trying to get her bearings. One thing at a time. Having a place to live would provide her with the opportunity to leave Bethany. At some point in her life, Jordan would have been terrified of the idea, now it filled her with relief.

She hoped Ellie wouldn't be too disappointed because Jordan needed some time to herself. Jordan didn't want to lose her. Truth be told she was falling in love with her. *How's that for terrifying?*

Jonathan Darby lived in a Victorian style building on the other side of town. It would have been easier to just walk the few blocks to his uptown office, but Jordan didn't mind the drive. It cleared her mind. The neighborhood reminded her of the one she'd be living in soon, quiet, private. She parked her car next to his jeep and walked up the stairs to his front door to ring the bell. A soft, melodic tone ensued.

Darby had worn a suit the other day, now had dressed in more comfortable slacks and a sweater. "I'm so sorry for messing up the appointment," she said by way of greeting. "It's late."

"That's no problem at all. Come on in. I have everything ready for you." He led her down the hallway into a large den with huge windows. Two sofas and an armchair sat around a coffee table, a small pile of printed papers and a couple of pens in the center of the tabletop.

"Take a seat. Why don't I run the details past you one more time, you look it over and sign?"

"Sounds good."

Jordan had educated herself with a quick check on Darby and his business. He had a great reputation and, from what she had learned, satisfied clients. It had to be enough. If she didn't sign tonight, she might not find the courage again. He let her read, leaving for another room as she skimmed over the contents. This was a game changer, she realized with excitement. She could be in her new home in a matter of days if everything went smoothly.

Darby returned with a small tray, carrying two glasses filled with about two fingers of an amber fluid. "I usually don't mix work with alcohol, but as you said it's late, and I believe this calls for a bit of celebration."

"Oh no, I can't. I still have to drive."

"Take a cab later, and I'll come pick you up tomorrow after I see the client," he suggested. "She'll be in before seven. That would work for you, right?"

It could if nothing happened overnight. In that case, Bethany would probably not be willing to give her a ride.

"Why not?" she said and accepted the glass. "Thank you."

"My pleasure. I'm glad to help. Your situation seemed...urgent."

Jordan signed her name at the bottom of the page before she took a sip of the whiskey. "That's one way to put it, yes. Mostly, I've been putting off the inevitable."

"You're a busy woman."

She picked up her glass again. "Busy is no excuse. I'm glad this is finally happening."

He gathered the papers, put them back on the table and sat next to her. Close. Jordan was reminded of the scene in his office, the touch lasting a bit too long, not all that innocent.

"To new beginnings," Darby said, before he leaned in to kiss her. Jordan indulged him for a moment long enough to realize she had a perfect opportunity to get herself into an even bigger mess, and that she didn't want to. Given the context of their shared drinking and her impending step into new freedom, it wasn't entirely unpleasant, just not pleasant enough.

She pulled back. "I'm sorry," she said, laughing a little, uneasy and embarrassed. "This is a bad idea."

Darby smiled. At least, he didn't take the rejection so badly. "I'm sorry too. This was going a little fast. A contract and a drink, let's leave it at that for the moment."

Okay, maybe she hadn't made herself clear enough. "I'm about to leave my partner. We've been together a little over nine years, and I'm not looking for a new relationship." The second part was little white lie, maybe, but he didn't need to know. "Besides, I don't date men. I'm sorry. I guess I should call that cab now. Thank you for everything."

"No problem. I'll still pick you up tomorrow?"

"That's fine, you don't have to. Just let me know if the owner accepted the offer, okay? I'll catch a ride at work and come pick up the car later if you don't mind."

"Sure, that's totally fine. Please, finish your drink. There's no point in wasting a good whiskey."

"I'm sorry about that. I need to go."

"Wait inside at least..."

"No, thanks."

To her relief, he didn't try any harder to change her mind, and the cab arrived within minutes. Jordan called Derek, asking him to pick her up in the morning.

"Don't ask," she warned.

He laughed good-naturedly. "I know your ways, Carpenter. I don't want to know."

"That sounds bad." She frowned. "What exactly do you mean by that?"

"Nothing. Enjoy your night. I'll see you in the morning."

Jordan leaned back into the seat, glancing at her watch. One of these days, sometime soon, she wouldn't have to come sneaking back into her own home—or have sex in a bathroom stall. In spite of these prospects being still in the future, she had to smile.

She had to go with her instincts more often. She had taken quite a few risks lately, and Jordan believed they would pay off. If only Ellie had a little more patience with her.

Ellie wasn't sure how to feel about the quick, messy, and so hot encounter in the restroom. Hot was what remained on her mind, even after going home in a cab, taking a shower and going to bed right away. Sleep was a faraway illusion, the residual effect of the alcohol and the memory made sure of that. Not that she minded replaying those moments, constant repeat, a welcome distraction from the previous mind movie that kept coming back on sleepless nights.

Even better to know that there was still a slight chance of making those fantasies come true, with someone else doing all the work like she had to now. She bit her lip like Jordan had earlier because those sounds would seem oddly loud in the stillness of the night. Maybe it wasn't life that owed her after all, and she'd been lucky to find someone who made her feel this complete—even when she wasn't present.

Chapter Ten

J ordan had expected questions, disdain, the usual. What she had not been prepared for was Bethany slapping her the moment she walked into the apartment.

"Whoa. What—"

"Where the hell have you been?"

"I told you, I—"

"Liar!" This time, she caught Bethany's wrist before her palm could connect with Jordan's cheek once more.

"Stop it. I had some errands to run. That's what I did. You want to have that talk now? Okay, let's do it."

"Why are you doing this to me?" Bethany's voice sounded slightly slurred, alerting Jordan to the fact that she hadn't been the only one drinking.

"Beth."

"No, you're listening to me for a change! When did I become so unattractive to you that you're willing to sleep with a man to get away from me?"

"That's not what happened!" Jordan stopped, unsure how to even start answering those questions, and how Bethany could have come to those conclusions. She was usually spot on, in an almost scary way. She had noticed something about Ellie right away, but maybe that was because Jordan was getting sick and tired of pretending.

However, Bethany had no way of knowing whom she had met tonight, unless she'd hacked into Jordan's phone. Technically, she could do that, but it was still illegal, and immoral. Not that Jordan had any ground to stand on when it came to morals. "What makes you think I did that?"

"I know," Bethany said darkly. "How stupid do you think I am?" She pressed a button on the phone, the answering machine. "You could at least tell them not to call here."

"Hi Jordan," Darby's voice sounded from the recording. "I just wanted to let you know I enjoyed our time very much, and I'm looking forward to seeing you again."

Jordan felt her jaw drop. What the hell was he thinking? Never mind the fact that she had been cheating, and was planning to leave Bethany, for real this time—this was out of line from a man whose only role in her life was to sell her a new home.

"All right, let's clear up the misunderstandings right now. I never slept with that guy, nor did I ever plan to. I honestly don't know why he left that message. I *am* in love with someone else though."

Bethany looked like she was the one who'd been slapped.

"Frankly, I don't know what else to tell you. I don't blame you, at all. In fact, I'm glad to take the blame, but I can't live like this anymore."

"What are you saying? You're taking the coward's way out after all? You're not even trying anymore?"

"Bethany, what do you want from me? I told you I'm in love with someone else. I'll stay with a friend, or go to a hotel, whatever."

Bethany followed her into the bedroom where Jordan pulled out a suitcase from the back of the closet. If Darby was to be believed, and she trusted him to be better at his job than he was at flirting, she would only have a few days to bridge.

"You are not doing this."

"Watch me. Now would you stop it?" Jordan snapped, irritated when Bethany took out every item she'd put inside the suitcase and threw them on the floor. "I'm leaving, okay? I'm doing you a favor. After this case is closed, you won't even have to see me anymore. I don't want the furniture. I just want to..."

"Keep screwing around?" Bethany suggested icily. "Because that's what you do, Jordan, and you're going to mess this up with her the same way. I'm already feeling sorry for the girl."

Jordan started picking up her clothes from the floor. There was no point in arguing. Worse, she could start to believe Bethany was right, and no one else would ever put up with her.

"If you want to go, go. Get out, now!"

Jordan barely ducked her keys.

"God, I can't stand to be in the same room with you anymore. This is how you thank me? Screw you! Not that you have to, I guess there'll always be one of your groupies around. Why don't you screw her?" Bethany asked, lowering her voice as if she was running out of breath. "Since you can't solve the damn case. That's at least one thing you're good at. Go, damn it!"

Jordan clenched her fingers around her keys, turning away to walk out of the room and the apartment. It wasn't so much the content of Bethany's words that rattled her rather than what they meant. She had suspected at times, but it was hardly between the lines anymore. Bethany hated her. It made her sad and a little nauseated to think she'd stayed around someone who couldn't stand her, for such a long time.

She cursed to herself when she remembered her car wasn't here—even if it had been, she was in no condition to drive.

❧

Sleep had finally embraced her, but it didn't seem that long until the doorbell jolted her out of it. For almost a full minute, Ellie sat up in her bed, her heart racing once more, but not for a good reason.

It could be important.

It could be him, coming back to finish the job he had screwed up in the first place. Get a freaking grip, she told herself. To come here would guarantee him world's stupidest criminal. She could check safely from inside the house.

By the time Ellie finally got to the door, she suspected the person to be gone, feeling slightly guilty at the thought that someone might need her help, bleeding on her doorstep...okay, now she was overreacting.

"Who's there?"

"It's Jordan."

Ellie allowed herself a moment of excitement, now wide awake, until she opened the door to her. From the dejected look on Jordan's face, she could tell the reason for her visit was neither a happy nor a sexy one. Their earlier encounter seemed unreal. She stepped back to let her in.

"What happened?"

"A lot happened. I'd rather not talk about it."

"Fine." Ellie closed the door behind her with a sigh. "Why should I be curious if you show up at my door at, what, three in the morning? Not like there's anything unusual about it."

"Ellie, please."

She studied her unexpected guest, wondering where to go from here. "Will you talk about it in the morning?"

"This was a bad idea. I shouldn't drag you into this. I just didn't know..." Jordan turned away, her posture unmistakable. Ellie embraced her from behind, holding on tight. While she had no idea what was going on, she could make an educated guess, and it seemed Jordan was barely holding it together. Someone had to.

"I'm right in the middle of it already," she whispered. "For once, don't run away. We'll figure it out."

"I never even asked you how you are doing. I'm so sorry. Now we know that it's the same guy..."

"We'll deal with it," Ellie said firmly. "As long as you are the only person showing up here in the middle of the night, I'm okay. You'll be too." She wasn't sure if Jordan believed her, but damn it, she'd keep on trying.

Ellie had indulged her far beyond any obligation. Truth be told, Ellie wasn't obliged to her in any way. The best Jordan could do for her was to avoid letting the complications in her own life spill over into Ellie's, but apparently, it was too late for that. She might have been shocked and confused about the outcome of her conversation with Bethany, but she knew, in the long run, that it had to come to this. A few hours of sleep had done wonders to clear her mind, and with Ellie snuggled against her, her body still sleep-warm, the temptation was too great. She was half awake when Jordan first kissed her, but when the sheet slipped to the floor, and her panties a moment later, she had Ellie's attention.

"What are you trying to do?" she asked, amused and breathless at the same time, as if it wasn't obvious.

"Thanking you for your hospitality," Jordan said, tracing the shape of her breast, then brushing her thumb over a nipple that perked under the touch. "Apologizing for leaving you hanging yesterday." Her hand moved lower, between Ellie's thighs. Ellie shivered, her skin warm and slick under Jordan's questing fingers.

"That might...work."

"Good." If being pressed, Jordan would have admitted she had ulterior motives that went beyond desire, like her need to restore some sort of balance. Last night, she needed to cry, to be held by someone who wouldn't ridicule her. It was no easy realization. She needed to present a more capable self. Well, even Bethany had admitted she was good at this—and this was the last thought she wanted to direct at her.

Ellie made it easy, trembling and moaning at the touch of Jordan's tongue against her sex, caressing, exploring. Jordan paused, looking up at her. "That means you'll forgive me?" she concluded, content with her progress.

"If you make it before the alarm..."

Jordan would never step away from a challenge.

⁂

"I might have a surprise for you later," she said when they were having breakfast. Ellie's face lit up with a smile.

"Another one?"

"Why not?"

"I'm intrigued," Ellie said, pouring milk into her coffee. "In all seriousness though...How much longer do you think Sergeant Bristol will let me stay on the task force when the progress is this slow? We know the killer is taking something from the scene, something that is or was of value to the victim. There's nothing connecting the bracelet with those coins unless they turn up on an auction website somewhere. I wanted to cross check with the chat users, see if something comes up in their profile."

"Good idea. As for your question, I don't know, but I want to widen the search. Maybe have another couple of officers on it. Go back to the All Colors, and Bethany...She needs to get more specific on the profile. It's not only your place on the task force that's up for discussion if we don't find Judy anytime soon."

"You think she's still alive?" Ellie asked, her gaze dark and somber.

"God, I hope so." Jordan didn't share that her hopes weren't all unselfish. She wanted the woman to escape the hell she was probably living in right now, but she also needed her to be alive and safe, because for once, Jordan needed to win. She cast a look at the clock on the wall, suppressing a curse. She hoped Derek didn't have a run in with an irate Bethany. In spite of her recent declarations, Jordan had dragged more people into the chaos that was her love life than necessary. All of this would be over soon.

Thinking of the unexpected turn of last night's event, she shuddered. She'd been lucky the night bus even got as far as it did, the ride making her feel like a teenager sneaking out of her parents' house. None of this bullshit anymore. She'd own a house soon.

"Yeah, me too," Ellie said. "If we leave right now, we might be able to get in before everyone else."

"I'm sorry, I have an appointment this morning. Would you mind if I leave after you and just close the door behind me?"

"Sure, no problem." Ellie went to get her jacket and purse. She stood in the doorway for a moment, regarding Jordan with concern. "Is everything really okay? I understand talking is not high on your list, but you know, if you want to, I'll listen." Jordan got up to step into her embrace.

"I know. Thank you. I have something to take care of, but don't worry. I promise I'll tell you everything."

"Okay then. I guess I'll see you at work?"

"Yeah. This won't take long."

After Ellie had left, she picked up her cell phone. Hopefully, Bethany would have calmed down enough to let her move.

Jordan wondered if she should give Darby a piece of her mind for making her life harder than it had to be with that message but decided to ignore it. After this deal, she'd never have to see him again.

He picked up after the first ring.

"Good morning, Detective," he said cheerfully. "I was just about to call you. Good news. She accepted your offer. You're now a homeowner. Would you like me to pick you up, or do you prefer to come by for the car later tonight?"

Oh, the damn car. She'd been so enthusiastic about her little secret she'd been drinking with her realtor. Inconvenient didn't even begin to describe it.

"If it's possible, I'd like to go now. Things didn't go quite as planned, and I need my car."

"No problem. Where are you now?" After yesterday's small incident, Jordan wasn't entirely comfortable sharing Ellie's address, so she named a hotel a couple of blocks away. She might even check in tonight, because after their last fight, she couldn't imagine spending another moment in the same apartment with Bethany.

Jordan had enough overtime accumulated to go in a bit later but hated to do so while this case was wide open. She consoled herself with the notion that everything would get better after this day.

Bethany was a professional. She'd refrain from further physical expression of her anger until after work. Maybe she had, like Jordan, gotten tired of fighting.

Ellie had suspected the workday wouldn't be entirely peaceful, but after last night—and this morning—she was more than willing to deal with the consequences. Sure, Jordan had issues.

It was hardly anything Ellie could complain about when she had been so ready to come between two people in a relationship. A highly dysfunctional relationship, true, but she hadn't known that in the beginning. A good night's sleep was still rare for her, and her thoughts kept revolving around the case and the missing woman's fate just the same.

They might have a shot at getting it right, on the job and in their tentative relationship.

She tried her best to stay away from Bethany though the profiler had adopted a polite mask and a tone that didn't reveal any of the trouble at home. Ellie wasn't sure if she could bring herself to feel sorry for her. She hadn't heard the whole story yet, but somehow she assumed it wouldn't be pretty.

As earlier discussed with Jordan, she began some deeper checks on the chat room users, and places where people interested in Judy Lawrence's hobby might be found. Jewelry. Coins. Isabel Hayes's only connection to the case was with Lori Gleason. She had no known relatives in the area. Ellie got up to study the map once more. The owner of the All Colors had been questioned as well. According to his statement, he had no knowledge of the dealings going on in his club. He had bought it less than six months ago after the building had been empty for almost a year. In the file, she found the name of the agency that had represented the previous owner, wondering why it sounded familiar.

It came back to her in a heartbeat. She remembered something Judy Lawrence's sister had told her. Meg had picked up some papers from the coffee table when Ellie had been at her house. *"I don't think she even looked at those, and now we don't know if she ever needs them,"* she'd said, tossing aside some flyers from the same realtor. Was it anything more but a coincidence? Judy had never met with the agency, and Meg would have hardly shared her frustrations about her sister with an employee, or would she?

Jordan hadn't made it to the department yet, but Ellie was sure she would want to know about it. She didn't manage to make the call.

"Officer Harding?" When she saw Bristol and Dr. Roberts standing in front of her desk, Ellie knew that the consequences of her actions, or Jordan's, had begun.

"Dr. Roberts tells me there's no need for this many people on the task force. I can't say I share the sentiment, but there's been a mass accident on Brooks. I want you to assist Robbins and McCarthy there."

"Is that necessary?" she asked, aware of Bethany's triumphant look on her. "I might have something—"

"Harding, if it wasn't necessary, I wouldn't ask you."

Ellie refrained from any further protest. Bristol hardly raised his voice, and when he did, he meant it. "No problem, sir."

"Good luck on your detective exam next year," Bethany said pleasantly. "I don't assume we'll meet again."

Ellie didn't bother to reply and left for her new assignment. *Don't worry about me, I've had lots of good luck lately.*

She called Jordan's cell phone in the squad car, but only reached her voicemail. "Hey. I've been sent to the accident on Brooks, but I think I found something that we should look into. The agency Meg wanted Judy to see about a new apartment—it's the same that sold the All Colors earlier this year. Okay. I think I'll see you later."

The thought filled her with excitement that was a lot stronger than her disappointment over being reassigned.

Darby had parked across from the hotel. "Finalizing a contract is always so much more than selling a building. It's a whole different life for most of my clients. I love that," he confessed after Jordan climbed into the passenger seat. To her relief, he didn't mention the call or the kiss. Maybe he'd left that strange message because he'd had more whiskey after her visit, not that alcohol was an excuse for ignoring the facts.

"I imagine it's rewarding," she offered vaguely.

"It truly is. Now let's go get your car. When do you think you'll move in?"

"Oh, I don't know, today? I kind of got thrown out."

He winced. "It was that urgent, huh? That's why you stayed at the hotel? I'm sorry to hear that. May I ask..."

Jordan shook her head. "Look, I appreciate your concern, but thanks to you, everything will be just fine. I won't be out on the streets until I close on the house either."

"Oh, come on," he said, chuckling. "Give me some credit. I didn't think a woman like you would have to spend a night out on the streets."

It was a somewhat dubious, backhanded compliment, so Jordan preferred not to answer to it. They drove in silence for a few minutes before he spoke. "I'm really sorry, going at this the wrong way. You said you're not ready. I respect that. I just want to help. Please let me know if you need anything, okay?"

"Sure," she mumbled. *I'm pretty sure I also came out to you, so don't sound so hopeful...*

"How are you going to celebrate getting into your new home?"

With blessed silence...She had promised Ellie though. If there was any time at all, she'd show her the outside of the house later. "I'm not sure there'll be much time for celebrating."

He nodded gravely. "It must be hard to be on the job at times like this, with time ticking away and there's nothing you can do."

"Oh, believe me, we are doing everything we possibly can," she returned, more defensive than she'd intended.

"Maybe you should take some time off, relax, and come back with a fresh perspective. I believe you're not the only one responsible for the outcome of the case. Am I right?"

Jordan stared straight ahead, relieved when Darby's residence came into view. "I'd rather not talk about it," she said.

"Okay." He parked the car next to hers, regarding her for a moment. "There's some info material I'd like to give you, contractors and designers we work with. I know you said you didn't want to make big changes at the moment, but maybe you'd like to do some updates once you feel more at home there. If you mention my name, they'll give you a good price."

"I don't have a lot of time. I really need to get back to work."

"This won't take long," he promised. "I have all of this in my office. I usually give a little package to clients, so they remember me." He winked.

"Oh well. It can't harm."

"Exactly. Come on in."

Jordan waited for him in the den, uncomfortably reminded of the previous night. Fortunately, after receiving the promo material, she wouldn't have to see Jonathan Darby again. She wondered if he habitually crossed lines with his clients. Jordan felt restless, eager to get the day going.

Checking her messages, she realized Ellie had tried to reach her. She frowned at the first part of the voicemail. Certainly, a lot of cops were working on that accident scene today, but there was hardly a reason to single out Ellie. Jordan could imagine whose doing this was. She wasn't quite sure what to do with the second, except...the vague connection to Judy. That was new.

Darby was taking his sweet time too. She walked the length of the tall bookshelves, holding leather-bound volumes, history, politics, architecture and more. Some figurines, glass, stone, female forms. She remembered the first time she'd walked into Darby's office in town, and the woman who had greeted her. Did he have more employees than that? Were they, or was he a little too interested in the private stories of his clients?

The All Colors. Judy Lawrence. Darby and his agency had been briefly on the radar of the investigators, but at that time, his connection had only been vague. They had concluded that Lori had only been held a short time in the couple's basement, the people who had used Darby's agency to find their dream home—one, as it turned out, that came with a starving, scared-to-death prisoner.

She jumped a bit when she saw him standing in the doorway, holding a colorful folder with his logo.

"You like those sculptures? They are very old," he revealed. "Medieval markets and fairs are my guilty pleasure. Of course, the architecture was fascinating too. A period that often isn't valued enough, in my opinion."

Jordan mostly associated the Middle Ages with the idea of witch trials. Maybe Ellie was really on to something. Meg had said the missing coins were medieval.

"I'm not an expert, but these look old to me. So, you find like-minded folks at those fairs, huh? You can sell or buy stuff, jewelry and other collectables?"

"Sometimes."

"Before I go...I was just wondering, does the name Meg Lawrence mean anything to you? I believe she once contacted you to make an appointment for her sister."

"True, but Judy never came."

"Oh...all right, that's all then. Thanks again. I better get going." Somewhere in the house, a phone rang, and he held out the papers to her.

"I'm afraid I have to take this. It was a pleasure working with you, Jordan. Enjoy your new home."

"Thanks. I can find my way out."

"Great," Darby said before he headed for his office once more.

In the hallway, Jordan opened and closed the front door, waited until the footsteps retreated and another door fell shut in the house. Jonathan Darby might just be what he let on, a talented realtor with a knack for the Middle Ages and an awkward flirt. If that was the case, he might forgive her, and no harm would be done.

If not...She was going to find out.

Chapter Eleven

F rom the moment Ellie arrived at the accident scene, she didn't have time to worry about the fact she still hadn't been able to reach Jordan, or what other ideas Bethany might have regarding her assignments.

A jackknifed 18-wheeler was blocking two lanes, and had caused a pile-up, involving at least twenty other vehicles from what Ellie could see. Ambulances had already left with the injured, but the massive traffic jam would last much longer.

She spent a lot of time trying to calm both worried and irate drivers who were stuck in the middle of it. A family of five was trying to get home, the children disappointed, because they had to cut their afternoon activities short. The oldest, a girl of about ten, stared at Ellie in fascination.

"Are you a real policewoman?" she asked, in awe.

"I swear. See my badge here?"

The girl's eyes grew wide. "Can I touch your gun?"

"No, you cannot." Ellie quickly changed the subject. "I'm sorry you don't get to go to the pool today, but it's really important the streets are all clear before everyone moves on." She got a grateful smile from the mother. The parents had obviously been less successful in trying to explain the circumstances.

"Chris pooped into his diaper," a younger girl declared, referring to the baby. "Ewww," the two older children echoed, making their parents and Ellie wince.

"Hang in there just a little bit," she said. "It won't take much longer."

Libby laughed when Ellie told her the story a few minutes later. "I guess that's not as glamorous as hanging out with Carpenter and her gang?"

"We were trying to find Judy Lawrence before he kills her," Ellie snapped. "That has nothing to do with glamour." She sighed when her sharp tone registered with her. "Sorry about that. I guess I'm a little on edge. Your day seems to have gone well so far."

Libby couldn't hide the proud smile. Instead of dubious attempts at entertaining children, she had made two drug-related arrests. "I just had to give them a stern look and they were falling over themselves telling me where exactly they hid their cocaine."

Ellie thought she needed a vacation. Maybe that was what she should have given herself after the attack, a time-out, and then come back refreshed. She couldn't turn back time now. Besides, sitting on a beach somewhere alone was nowhere near as thrilling as those stolen moments with Jordan. Not so stolen anymore. From today on, they'd belong to her.

With new resolve, she walked the length of the vehicles. Jordan had been so determined earlier this morning, regarding the case and sorting out her relationship. Ellie was looking forward to seeing her later.

The driver of a Ford stared straight ahead as she walked by. Not everyone in this traffic jam was keen on talking to the police. He also had a couple of young kids, preschool age, in the backseat. Ellie took in the dirt on the side of the car, and the man's rugged clothing. Neither was in itself a clear indicator that something was wrong, but something about this vehicle raised her suspicion, and she decided to run a quick check.

"Good afternoon," she said to the man, her tone friendly and polite.

He didn't look at her, but beads of sweat were forming on his forehead. "Afternoon, Ma'am."

"I'm sorry for the delay. The lanes will be open in about twenty, thirty minutes. The kids are okay back there?"

"Why wouldn't they be?"

Two pairs of eyes stared back at her anxiously. That didn't have to mean anything. Some parents taught their children to look at the police with suspicion. Or they were intimidated by the uniform and too young to understand what it meant.

"No reason," Ellie said. "Sir, could I see some identification, please?" She watched closely as he opened the glove compartment. The minute distraction of both children starting to cry was enough. The next moment he had a gun pointed at her.

"Come in if you want to talk to them," he said, sounding desperate. His hands clutching the gun were shaking.

⁂

Jonathan Darby was still on the phone. What the hell was she doing, sneaking around in the man's house? She should go back, see if they had anything on him that would be enough to convince the DA to issue a warrant. Jordan sighed. Not likely at this point. It was peculiar that he knew at once Meg was Judy's sister, but other details had surfaced already. A complete media blackout was tough to implement.

She didn't have much of a choice.

So far, the murders had been executed in a chaotic way, not well planned all around. He might not leave clues lying around for her, but there had to be something. A quick and inconclusive search of the kitchen and dining area brought her back to the den and its huge shelves. He could have met Judy at one of those fairs. Lori—her husband's business was loosely related to real estate. He could be one of those unidentified dates in the chat room, and without a doubt Darby's profession provided him with lots of information regarding possible hideouts.

Then again, for someone with this much opportunity to hide the victims, he seemed sloppy. Did that mean he wanted to be found? She leaned back against the shelf, assured that the phone conversation a few rooms away was still going, trying to think of an excuse why she was still here and why she would like to see the floor plan of this house...when she felt herself fall backwards.

The shelf was moving. Whether or not Jonathan Darby had something to hide like skeletons in his closet, or a kidnap victim somewhere in this house, one thing was for sure: He did have a secret room.

Jordan tried to curb her fascination when she stepped into an even bigger library. She didn't have much time as it was, and if he caught her here, she would have even more explaining to do. There was a huge table with armchairs around it in the center of the room, shelves lining two of the walls. No window in here. The lamp was probably powered by a motion detector, switching on as soon as someone entered the room.

Thick carpeting blocked out the sound of her footsteps. Unfortunately, she couldn't hear him talking on the phone here either.

If there was anything to be found in here, where did she have to look? Behind a painting? Would she make a fool out of herself? There was no cell phone reception in here, so calling for backup was out of the question at the moment.

Jordan found the door behind some heavy drapes, purely decorative since there were no windows. One of them covered up more than wall. The moment she made one step forward, the light went out in the room behind her, and she nearly fell through the square opening in the floor. Holding onto the wall, she was trying to catch her breath as her eyes adjusted to the darkness, and she could make out the contours of the open trap door, and a ladder leading down.

A small sound broke the heavy silence that had engulfed her since she'd stepped into the library. And another. She had the choice of backing out of this right now and risk running into him or moving forward. The person she suspected to be below the trap door might not have that much time. If she went down there, a confrontation was unavoidable. Jordan straightened her shoulders. Her cell phone might be useless down there, but her gun wasn't.

Getting a possibly injured woman out of there and to her car before Darby realized Jordan had never left his house—piece of cake. Tonight, it might all be over.

With that motivation, she carefully set her foot on the wooden ladder.

The room down here was bigger than she had expected, with a tiny opening on the far wall that left in enough light to illuminate a gruesome scene. Down here, it was hard to believe that it was still daylight outside, only a beam of it finding its way in. It had to be enough.

"Judy!"

For a moment, she feared the woman slumped over in the chair was already gone, but then her eyelids fluttered, and she flinched under Jordan's careful touch.

"It's okay. I'm with the police. We're going to get you out of here now." That might be a premature promise, Jordan realized when she became aware of the heavy chains that held Judy Lawrence to the chair. Any attempt to move them caused sounds of pain.

Jordan recalled the autopsy reports of Campbell and Hayes, bruises, broken bones. "I'm so sorry," she whispered. "This will be over soon. I promise."

The woman's bitter laugh startled her. "That's what *he* said."

"Work with me. I've got my car here. We'll get you to the hospital in no time."

"What if he comes back?"

"I've got this too," Jordan said, pointing to her gun.

A lock held the restraints in place. Getting to the key was impossible at the moment, so she had to work around it. Unfortunately, this wasn't the movies. She didn't have a hairpin at hand, nor was anything suitable simply lying around. Maybe the buckle of her belt would do. Okay, it was a little like in the movies. Jordan hoped she would come out the hero and not the expendable, careless character who got herself killed.

Ellie didn't have magic words. All she had was the desire to get out of this situation with everyone alive at the end, the two children, her, and the man who was still training the gun on her in unsteady hands.

"This isn't going to work," she said, amazed at how calm her tone was. Ellie wasn't feeling calm, more like she was suffocating. Even with the windows rolled down, the air was stuffy. Her uniform felt hot and uncomfortable. "I checked your vehicle. In a minute or so, my colleagues will realize something is wrong, and...look ahead. The lane is still blocked. They won't let us out of here. Let me help you," she added quickly, before the man could get the idea his situation was completely hopeless. It didn't look good, but Ellie didn't want him to think that using his gun was an option. "Let's take a look at what the problem is, and how we can solve this. What's your name?"

"You're a cop. You can get us out of here."

"I can do my best to keep this from getting out of hand, okay. Look at those kids, they're scared. They are yours, I assume?"

"Yes, I'm their father, and no one's going to take them away!"

Okay, she was on to something here. "Who wants to take them away?"

"My ex-wife and her jerk of a boyfriend, that's who," the man said. "Not going to happen, I'm telling you that. He wants to be a dad, but they already have a dad."

"Yeah, and currently he's scaring the hell out of them. Look at them."

She saw a hint of uncertainty on the man's face. "Put that gun away, please. I'm sure you can still work something out with your ex. If you keep this up, it's likely you'll never get to see your children again. It's not too late. You cooperate, and I will testify on your behalf."

"You're just saying that."

"I want these kids to be safe, okay? Don't you?"

He looked in front of them, behind them, the road around them still packed with vehicles, nowhere to go. Then he took in the pair of wide-eyed, frightened children in the backseat. Ellie held her breath.

"My name is Harold," he said, before he handed the gun to Ellie, leaned forward and started crying, the boy and girl joining in. Ellie wanted to cry too, but she supposed that could wait until the situation was under control.

On the bright side, she'd be able to testify that Harold had indeed had a change of heart, but the fact that he kidnapped his own children, wouldn't make it easy for him.

"It will be okay," she said, thinking that a too vague and general statement wasn't the same as a bold lie—or was it?

Judy was fading fast. The air was stifling and hot. She was probably thirsty and hurting, drifting in and out of consciousness, but finally, the chains fell. Jordan shuddered at the feel of blood on her hands.

"You'll see, we'll have you out of here soon. It's not going to be long now. Can you stand?"

Supporting almost all of the woman's weight, Jordan wondered how she'd manage to haul her up those narrow rungs, especially without making her injuries worse. She had to try, even risking that Darby might be waiting for them on the other side of the door. "We've got to go," she said firmly. "Do you remember the library room upstairs?" There was no answer. "Once we're out of there, I'll have reception, and I can call someone. We have to get up there."

She wasn't sure if Judy had understood her until she heard a small whispered "okay."

"Okay. Let's do this."

The way up seemed to take an eternity. In her condition, even Judy's petite frame was heavy. She could move, slowly, with lots of pain. It hurt Jordan that she had to add to it. There was no other way. Today, both of them would go home, and she'd be able to tell Ellie that she was safe too.

One agonizing minute after the next ticking by. He had to know she was still in the house when he saw her car. Finally, they reached the top step and the door to the library, where the light came back on. Judy flinched violently.

The room looked like Jordan had left it. He hadn't been in here yet. Could they be so lucky? "We're almost there," she said, a heartbeat before Judy collapsed in her arms. "Oh no, not now. I need you to stay with me, okay? Judy!"

She had to half-drag her across the room. Fortunately, she hadn't locked herself in. The shelf moved just as easily as when she'd come in. Almost free. If necessary, she'd get Judy all the way to her car and then...

"Jordan," a voice behind her said. "Where do you think you're going?"

Chapter Twelve

"I heard what happened earlier. I'm really sorry."

Ellie looked around her, quickly determining that she and Bethany were alone in the locker room. Oh well. After the recent events, she felt pretty much fearless. No, that wasn't true. She was still all jittery inside. That had to be the reason why Bristol had sent her home. He seemed to have a knack for seeing those things.

"I'm okay. I'm glad in the end, he didn't want the kids to get hurt." She wondered if she could risk asking the profiler if she'd heard from Jordan. Ellie hadn't seen her since the morning.

"Good job talking the guy down," Bethany said. "You have a bright future in this department. Everyone says so."

"Thanks." *I guess.*

"If you don't mind a word of advice though, that's what you should focus on. Your career. Sleeping with the wrong person can get you in trouble."

So much for avoiding the subject. "With all due respect—"

Bethany laughed. "Why is it that people always say that when they couldn't care less?"

"Did Jordan come in yet? There's something I need to tell her. About the case."

"Really?" Bethany narrowed her eyes at her. "You've been waiting all day to share this?"

"I tried to reach her. I couldn't, and besides, you made sure I wasn't anywhere near the task force today." She held up her hands in defense. "Forget about it. I'm sorry I said anything. It's probably not important." Ellie would be the judge of that. She'd see if she could have a minute with Henderson before she went home. All she wanted at the moment was to evade a pointless exchange. Jordan had made her decision, whatever Bethany thought about it. "Have a good day." Okay, she probably didn't need to do that.

"Don't fool yourself," Bethany said behind her back. "Jordan will come back to me. She always does when she gets tired of her silly little affairs."

The insult in her words hit home as it probably meant to do, but Ellie refused to reward it with an answer and left Bethany standing.

Derek Henderson wasn't at his desk. Ellie stood, indecisive, for a moment. She'd try to reach him later if she didn't hear from Jordan.

She wondered if the silence had to do with the surprise Jordan had talked about earlier.

"No, come on. You don't think I'm stupid, do you? Let me have that gun and your cell phone, please."

She had no choice. Judy leaning on her heavily had hindered a quicker reaction. Damn. This was bad.

"You have a backup piece, right?" He laughed as if he just made a good joke. "They always do on TV, fooling the bad guy. Not that it's what I am. Right, Judy? We discuss some important matters down there."

No answer from Judy, but her condition spoke volumes. Jordan swallowed her anger. It would do her no good at the moment.

"I can see that, but she's not feeling so good. I need to take her to the hospital. Can you let me do that?"

"Can you shut up?" he yelled, startling her so badly that Judy slipped in her grip.

"Okay. I'm sorry. I'm sure we can talk about this."

"Oh, we will talk, Jordan, no doubt about that. Now let her go, so we can get started." Sensing her hesitation, he added, "I have a gun, and I can shoot both of you before you even blink, so if you think about trying something stupid—don't."

Timing. Ellie had tried to reach her before. Her colleagues would start to wonder as she hadn't once checked in with work yet, and Ellie had already asked her about Darby's agency. All she had to do was keep him talking.

"If we leave her here for now, is that okay?" If she was lucky, Judy could find a way to get out. It would all work out. She just had to keep him from shooting anyone. If she could lower the woman gently onto the carpet and...get to her ankle holster...

The red-hot pain made her stagger, consuming her before she could even locate it, and the unconscious woman slipped from her grasp. He had stabbed her thigh.

Darby was quick tackling her to the floor, cold metal pressed against the back of her neck.

"Oops," he said, his voice dripping with contempt. "I guess I lied. It was a knife instead. Do you want me to use it again?"

With his weight bearing down on her, the pain making her dizzy and her voice drowned out by the thick carpet, she couldn't give much of an answer.

"I can't hear you." Just for emphasis, he fisted his hand in her hair and pulled back sharply. Her vision started to grey out. Timing, the word seemed to mock her right now.

Eventually, she'd be able to talk and reason with him. She had to.

"No. I said no." She didn't think the blade had cut that deep, but damn it, it hurt. She could feel the blood trailing down her leg. "You don't...you don't have to do that."

"Will you accept your punishment?"

He leaned in close, and it took her a moment to realize he was tracing the shell of her ear with his tongue. Her body revolted, but she forced herself to stay still.

He found the ankle holster next. "I guess TV is good for something. I'm so glad we're finally getting somewhere. I'm sorry, Jordan, this might hurt a bit. You should have thought about the consequences of your actions sooner." It might have been his intention to knock her out, but she managed to dodge the blow, gasping when the movement made pain shoot up her injured leg. She couldn't escape the second—or the third, and the darkness that followed.

❦

"Damn. She hasn't checked in all day?" Henderson looked worried.

Bethany shrugged. "Jordan is like that sometimes. Not to say she's irresponsible, but you must know that about her. She needs to take her time and mull things over, and most of the time, she comes back with a good idea. She was probably following some leads of her own."

Ellie hadn't made it home yet. She found Bethany's lack of concern disconcerting.

"Oh, come on, she would have answered one message!" She ignored the warning looks from both Bristol and Henderson. "You might have worked with her before, but not everyday like these guys. Jordan is not like that!"

"You know her so well," Bethany said, her voice dripping with sarcasm. "She texted me though, said that we'd talk later. I guess she got cold feet."

"Then where the hell is she?" Ellie didn't care if the course of the conversation was slightly awkward for the two men present, Jordan's partner and their boss.

"I don't know. We'll find out soon. What are you still doing here anyway?" Bethany asked.

"I hate to say it, but she's right," Bristol said. "I wasn't joking when I said I wanted you to go home."

"Sir..."

"I mean it, Harding. Go home."

"Don't worry," Henderson told her. Exchanging a glance with Bristol, he followed Ellie outside the room. "We'll figure this out. I'll keep you updated, I promise."

"You didn't want to say that in front of her, did you?"

"No."

"I know Jordan's dealing with a lot of...stuff right now," Ellie said. "I need to know she's okay. You'll check on that real estate agency again?"

"First thing tomorrow," he said. "The sergeant is right. You should be home."

"Yeah. With all that unpleasantness, I nearly forgot about the guy who waved a gun in my face."

"You did well. Take some time to relax," he advised. "I'll call you as soon as I know more."

"Thank you."

On her way home, Ellie drove past Jordan's apartment. Since Bethany was still at the department, she was a minor concern at the moment. She drove around the building, noticing that Jordan's car was not in its spot. Where was she? Ellie wanted to tell her she didn't care much about a surprise. She wanted to be sure she was safe, because bad things happened, every day, without warning.

She assumed that Henderson and his colleagues would take the necessary measures if they thought something was wrong. Ellie was unnerved by how they had relegated her to the sidelines. She should call Libby or Kate and see if one of them—or both—were up for a girls' night out.

Spending all night home alone would drive her crazy.

Ellie was glad to find Kate at home and ready to have some girl talk over a drink or two. She also had an idea what would be the subject of said girl talk: Kate had been present during the search in Gleason's house, when they'd found the maps. Maybe there was something they could figure out together.

If only Jordan called.

❦

Daylight. She hadn't seen daylight in forever, or so it seemed to Judy when she managed to open her eyes. The sun was setting, judging from the play of shadows of the floor. How many days? The surface was unusually soft. She moved her hand a fraction, wincing at the pain.

Pain. Cold and heat alternating. His eyes. Her heart was racing, fragments coming back to her, all of them hinting at the same terrifying picture.

She had to get out of here.

She didn't know if she could make it, to her feet, let alone the door, but she had to try. Otherwise, the pain would never stop. She had to try. For her. For...what was her name? She remembered her crying, all the time. Lori.

They had to find Lori.

She stifled a scream when she put weight on her foot, stumbling to her knees again. The next time, she got to her feet, holding herself up against the wall. Looking back, Judy saw blood on the floor, but she didn't know if it was hers.

Get out.

She couldn't afford to let her attention stray. If he found her, the punishment would be worse than anything. The punishment for those who didn't learn was death. Biting her lip hard enough to draw blood, she moved further, until her fingers curled around the intricate wrought-iron pattern of the front door.

"I hate it, really. I don't want to think about another woman that way." Obviously, there was something Ellie had to get off her mind first. After the second beer, it was a little easier, though Kate wasn't overly sympathetic.

"You're jealous," she stated.

"Of course I am, but that's not the point."

Kate laughed. "I think it's exactly the point. I mean...Yeah, she's been a bit of a bitch, but she's kind of entitled, don't you think? Her girlfriend is sleeping with someone else. You, to be correct."

"Do you have to say it like that?" Ellie asked miserably, amusing her friend even more.

"How else do you want me to say it?"

"Oh, please, shut up."

"Now, don't be rude. I understand. You've had to deal with a lot of shit lately, and it's normal you were looking for a little distraction. The problem is involving someone who has issues of their own. I assume."

Ellie didn't tell Kate that her assumptions were too close for comfort but changed the subject instead.

"You were on the scene that day. Why does he hide these things in the threshold?"

"Maybe Gleason didn't," Kate said. "Maybe someone was trying to set him up."

"He did know things though. He was somehow involved."

Kate looked thoughtful. "I don't know as much about the case as you do, but he seemed pretty crazy to me, Gleason, I mean. He might have contacted someone to harm his wife, but that person is certainly cleverer than he was. Someone who knows about these old hiding places."

"Yeah." While Ellie knew that Derek Henderson cared about Jordan, and he would follow up on the lead Ellie had told him about, she was still restless, even after two beers.

There was no message from either Jordan or Derek.

"I'm sorry, I...I need to check on something. I'll pay for your cab, or you can come with me." One thing she couldn't bring herself to do was leave Kate without knowing if she'd get home safely. Too much had happened already.

"As long as you promise me you won't get into trouble...I'll be okay. I'll just call Jensen to pick me up...come on, like you hadn't figured that out yet."

Ellie thought ruefully she hadn't been that good at seeing what was right in front of her lately. She would find out where Jordan was and go from there. Bethany might be rightfully pissed at her, but her earlier dismissal was revealing. She didn't seem to care all that much.

Ellie waited until Jensen arrived and left for Jordan's apartment building once more. What if she was home already? Much as Ellie hoped this could be the case, she doubted it, her fear for the possible scenarios growing.

With consciousness returning, she immediately started to flail, and almost passed out again before she could regain enough control to breathe through her nose, slowly. Her leg was on fire, her head pounding, but with each moment, Jordan became more aware that her problems were bigger than that. While the cut might not be life-threatening, the strain on her arms and legs reminded her of it with every pained heartbeat. The bastard had strung her up by her wrists, only her toes touching the stone floor.

Damn him and his medieval fantasies.

Jonathan Darby stood in a corner, smoking a cigarette, watching her with the fascination one might give a bug under a microscope. She had dealt with people like him in an interrogation room, never in their favorite hiding place where they had the upper hand. For a moment, the fear enveloped her, stole her breath even more. Time was ticking by as she struggled to get her bearings, while he kept observing her silently.

"I'm so glad you're with me, Jordan," he said eventually. "I've been looking forward to this. I believe you might benefit a lot more from our lessons than Judy did."

She was trying to force the question out before she remembered the duct tape, her struggles amusing the killer in front of her.

"Don't worry about Judy. For now, you should worry about yourself."

When he stepped closer, she kept an eye on the gleaming end of his cigarette, tensing in anticipation of more pain, another layer over the ever-present ones, but he tossed it to the floor and put it out with his shoe.

"I'm going to tell you how this works. I'm not a monster." His lips curved into a smile at her expression. "Yes, I know you believe that, but it's not true. In fact, all I want is to help you get on a better path in life, be a better person. I know it's tough, but I'm here to help you. You don't want to continue your life as a lying, cheating whore, do you?"

He ripped off the duct tape, his words still resonating with such force she forgot about the pain for a heartbeat—but only a heartbeat.

"Is that why you killed the women? You didn't like the way they lived their lives, and you thought it was up to you...to stop them?" She coughed, wishing she could get anywhere near the bottle of water on the table behind him.

"I know you have many questions. I'll try to answer them as we go along." He brushed his hand over her cheek, making her skin crawl, and despite the heat in the room, she shuddered. "The truth is, no one wants to live like that, but some of them were stubborn. It's not my fault they didn't listen. They died. It happens." He leaned closer. "I have a good feeling about you. I think we're going to get along well."

Jordan was tempted to spit in his face, but she was aware that everything depended on her ability to keep him talking. He had never killed right away, so she did stand a chance. Angering him, as long as she was the one in cuffs, was not a good idea.

"Maybe. You should know I'm not cheating on anyone. I broke up with my girlfriend. That's why I needed a new place, remember?"

He smiled. "Then let's make sure you'll never do it again, shall we?"

"Hey, what the hell are you—"

He had ripped her shirt open, for what purpose, was unclear as there was no way to get it over the cuffs without opening them, which he clearly didn't intend. She had to keep her mind clear off worst-case scenarios, although they became more likely by the minute. Her pants came down next. She couldn't help the pained gasp as the fabric dragged over the cut, tears pooling in her eyes against her will.

"Hey, don't cry yet," Darby said, patting her shoulder. "This isn't too bad, but we have to clean it up a bit anyway. You don't want to get it infected."

What I don't want is to be here, with a psychopath who thinks he needs to educate me.

"How considerate of you."

"Don't be sarcastic. I'm not the one who screwed up, remember."

He did a fairly quick and efficient job of cleaning the cut, but her relief was short-lived when he grabbed the small bottle, whose contents she could identify by the unmistakable smell. "Oh no, I don't think that's necessary..."

For a moment, she feared she'd throw up on him, but it didn't happen. When he had finished bandaging the cut, she was drenched in sweat though, trembling hard. She could handle it. She had to. As long as he didn't get any other ideas, she'd bide her time until her colleagues found her.

"Welcome to your lesson," Darby said.

The tables would turn soon.

Chapter Thirteen

S till no message, and no sight of Jordan's car, which meant she hadn't returned. Ellie stood in front of the empty parking space until the futility of her actions hit home with her—and the possible omissions. Was she the only one who was worried sick by now? Sure, both Henderson and Bethany knew Jordan better. It was hard to tell whether they didn't care, or they thought it wasn't necessary to keep Ellie in the loop—about anything. The latter was probably closer to the truth.

Bethany was a professional. If she thought anything was wrong, she wouldn't be so petty to let jealousy get in the way, not if Jordan's life was in danger—or would she? Ellie still wondered about the connection between Gleason and the man who had attacked her, and most likely kidnapped the other women. How had they found one another?

"What are you doing here?"

Jumping at the unexpected voice behind her, Ellie spun around, facing Bethany who looked more exhausted than angry. Hopefully that meant she could make a quick escape.

"I'm sorry, I don't mean to bother you. I'm just worried about Jordan." Ellie had expected irritation or disdain, but Bethany's real reaction was almost worse.

"It's all your fault," she claimed, her cool façade crumbling. "God, did you really have to do that? If something happened to Jordan, it's on you. She's never been so distracted."

"This is not helping. I better go."

"That's right, run away, why should you take any responsibility, right? You're doing the best you can to destroy a good relationship, but hey, nothing wrong with that!"

"I wasn't…I'm sorry." Ellie raised her hands. "I wanted to make sure she's okay. Sorry." If she was repeating herself, that was because every word between them seemed like walking on a minefield. Concern for Jordan was the safest possible subject.

"Don't you think I want that too? Henderson is the last who heard from her since she ran out on me. Imagine how that felt when he showed up on my doorstep this morning, and I had to come up with an explanation, because the one thing I didn't want to tell him was that she spent the night with you?"

At least, with Bethany losing her composure like this, Ellie could be fairly sure she did care, in her own way—which didn't solve the problem they had in the first place.

"What did Henderson say? Are they doing anything?" She sounded equally as desperate, Ellie realized.

Bethany shrugged. "The usual. You know as well as I do, it's tricky this early, especially with someone who has a history of running when things get complicated. We can't dig into her finances yet, but if she doesn't come home tonight, I might go there rather sooner than later."

Ellie nodded. She didn't want to prolong this conversation unnecessarily, but she didn't think she could wait another night. "Did Detective Henderson say anything about that real estate agency?"

"He's going to check it out tomorrow. Now…would you mind?"

"Of course. I'll see you tomorrow." Ellie stopped herself short of saying 'good night' when it was so clear neither of them would have one. She walked a few steps and then stopped.

Bethany groaned. "What now?"

"Jordan said she had a surprise for me."

This was no time to walk on eggshells. Ellie was scared Jordan's troubles might be worse than hiding from her relationship issues.

"Oh my God. What do I have to do to make you leave me alone?"

"Think about it. Somewhere, someone must have seen her today."

"Are you for real? I don't want to discuss this with you. Ever. Go home."

This time, Ellie obliged, but she was far from giving up.

❧

"Ellie? What the hell are you doing here?"

She had to be doing something wrong, greeted like this for the second time within a few hours.

Ellie wiped a hand over her face and smoothed down her hair, fairly embarrassed that she'd fallen asleep at her desk. When the reason registered with her, the fact Henderson had caught her like this was the least of her concerns.

"Did you hear from Jordan?"

Outside, the day was dawning. It was an early start for Jordan's partner as well. He shook his head. "I'll see the realtor in a bit. Maybe Jordan went to visit him. Coffee?"

"Yes, please. Thank you. Is that true?" she asked, following him into the break room. "What Bethany said about Jordan? I didn't get the impression she'd do something like this, go away and not let anyone know, even on the job. I am scared."

Henderson regarded her thoughtfully, as if he needed a moment to weigh his words.

"I am worried too," he admitted. "Please, don't get this the wrong way, but you don't know her very well. Jordan is a good friend, and a better cop, but she has her own way of doing things. With excellent results that most of us can be jealous of. Nonetheless it wouldn't be the first time. I can't speak for Dr. Roberts, and I don't know how much Jordan has told you." He sighed. "I shouldn't discuss this with you."

Why not? Ellie bit back the sharp response, knowing it would do no good, though she was tempted. *Why not, when I seem to be the only one who gives her any credit that goes beyond lip service?*

"Yeah, whatever. When you talked to the guy, let me know?"

"Sure. Look, I'm sorry you had to leave the task force. Next year, things might be easier for you. Keep up the good work, and you'll be moving upstairs soon enough."

"Thanks."

"You're welcome," he said. "Talk to you later."

Ellie sat back, wondering who else she knew might have a desire to punish a cheating partner.

He walked past the agency—it wasn't opening time yet—having a hard time to keep from whistling as the sliding doors of the police department opened to him. He hoped to be able to see Jordan Carpenter's empty desk. It might not work that way, but he felt ecstatic, even after a long night, and another loss.

He didn't think Judy would make it far, and if they found her body, the police wouldn't be able to tell more than they had with the other women. He always took care to keep the scene clear of too many hints and clues. He would need another scapegoat though, soon, but first there was something else on his list.

Jonathan Darby thought of the woman who had been convinced she could stop him, and currently wasn't having such a good time after the early lessons. When he left her this morning, she'd been a lot less defiant than when they got started. He'd let her down not too gently, and she curled up on the floor, shivering, the heavy chains not giving her a lot of leeway. She was almost ready to acknowledge her faults.

"Good morning. Jonathan Darby," he said to the female officer at the front desk. "I'd like to speak to Detective Carpenter, if possible?"

Her eyes widened, then she said, "Wait a minute please." He stepped back politely while she was talking on the phone, already anticipating the course of events that would follow. A moment later, a man in a suit and a petite woman in uniform joined him.

Ellie Harding had no idea how lucky she'd been.

The man introduced himself as Detective Henderson, Jordan's partner.

"Detective Carpenter isn't here?" he asked, acting surprised. "We had an appointment this morning. She didn't show up and I couldn't reach her, so I thought I'd try here."

Henderson exchanged a look with Officer Harding.

"When did you make that appointment?"

"Two days ago. We closed a deal for a house, and I was supposed to give her some papers. She hinted that the move was kind of urgent. We were trying to expedite things for her. I'm surprised she didn't call me." He paused for dramatic effect. "Did anything happen?"

"We don't know yet," Henderson said. "Mr. Darby, can I talk to you for a moment? I'd like to hear more about this house sale."

"Um...sure, I guess that's okay. Usually, those details would be confidential, but if she's in trouble, I want to help. Wow. This was not what I expected."

"Good. Please follow me." Another meaningful look to Harding. "That would be all, Officer."

She didn't look happy, but Jonathan silently assured her: *Don't worry. I won't forget about you.*

The big secret. Jordan had bought a house, and obviously, Bethany didn't know about it. Not that this gave Ellie any advantage over her, because she hadn't known either until a minute ago. What did it all mean? Darby, the owner of the real estate agency, had been under scrutiny before, with the house where Lori was found, and recently, because Meg had made an appointment with his company for Judy.

She hoped Derek would think of asking him for a list of employees, then she slapped a hand against her forehead. Henderson was a seasoned detective, not a wannabe like Ellie at this point. Of course, he would remember the details.

She tried to make herself invisible behind her computer when she saw Bethany walking in, her immaculate appearance revealing nothing about the near meltdown Ellie had witnessed the previous night.

It was hard to figure out the woman. Why was she holding on to Jordan, when she didn't seem to have that much respect for her? Emotional blackmail? Revenge? Both she and Derek seemed to be privy to secrets Ellie had no idea of. Maybe Jordan had planned on telling her some time. Maybe the house was the surprise, a place where they could be together without the presence or judgment of another person?

Judgment.

Revenge.

Punishment.

Ellie knew without a doubt the person who had attacked her was male, but his connection to Gleason suggested that sometimes, he carried out "punishment" for those who wanted to get back at their spouses.

Bethany?

She certainly had all the means to hide her traces, but she wouldn't team up with a murderer for something this petty—would she? Ellie shook her head to herself. Kate might be right to say that her judgment was clouded by jealousy.

She was wondering what Derek and the realtor had to discuss this long.

After they left the interview room, Darby passed by her desk.

"Have a good day, Officer…Harding it is?" He smiled before he turned to walk away.

A shudder ran down her spine before she could identify where it was coming from. He had overheard her name earlier, no need to get paranoid.

She had more important things to do.

⁂

It took her a while to break through the stronghold of shock. Numbness meant being wrapped in a cocoon of nothingness, where there was no pain or consideration of what he might do next. She couldn't afford to stay there. Numbness would get her killed.

Apparently, the chains could be straightened—or the opposite—with some kind of mechanism, but she didn't have enough leeway to get to it, manipulate it in any way.

"I'll be back," he'd said. "I promise. We can continue all afternoon."

That was part of the problem, really, he wouldn't say what exactly he expected her to do or say. Her only way to pass was to stay alive. Even though it wasn't cold in the room, it took forever for the shakes to finally abate.

She was hyper aware of her scarcely dressed state, every minute he was in the room with her. Jordan knew it was part of the tactic, to keep her off balance. What she didn't know was where he planned to go from there, and the fear was part of his game. He was putting on a show. She could do the same.

Judy came to in the same place she'd curled up some time the previous night, woken by the rays of light coming in through the cracks in the walls of the old barn. She was confused and hurting. She had no idea where she was, or why.

She looked at her wrists, crusted over with blood, dizziness assaulting her.

What had happened to her? Then again, if she was the one hiding, did that mean she had done something illegal? She couldn't think clearly. She was so hungry. Food, any kind of food, was the priority. Water. Judy had dragged herself back to the door, set a foot outside when she realized the tunic over her underwear was all she was wearing.

Nowhere was safe.

Chapter Fourteen

"Jordan said she had a surprise for me. I think she was talking about the house." At this point, Ellie was past any feeling of embarrassment or shame. "I didn't mention it before, because I thought it wasn't important, but now—"

"It is still not important," Bethany said coolly. "You're as unprofessional as Jordan running away in the middle of this, but I'm beginning to understand why. She signed the contract and then realized what she had done. This is not something you can get out of so easily."

"She signed the contract because she wanted to get away from you!"

"Sergeant, I fail to comprehend why Officer Harding is still part of this investigation, when her private interest in my partner is clearly all she has to offer."

Derek Henderson winced.

"With all due respect, Dr. Roberts, Detectives Carpenter and Henderson requested Officer Harding, and if I remember correctly, she has done her job as expected. All else, I agree, doesn't belong here—from either of you. I'd like you all to go back to work now and find Detective Carpenter. If she was following a lead, I'm certain it was legit. You figure out everything else on your own time."

BARBARA WINKES

To Ellie's surprise, Bethany followed her all the way to the squad car and sat in the passenger seat next to her.

"You heard the sergeant. I have a job to do, and I believe so do you."

Bethany sighed, but she didn't make any move to leave.

"What?" Ellie snapped.

"I believe Jordan might have taken off with some guy. I know, that doesn't make either of us look good."

This was the last thing Ellie needed to hear after the night she'd had. "Remember what you said to me yesterday? I'm going to have to ask you the same thing. Go."

"She met with him. He called our home and left a message, about how much he enjoyed himself. As usual, Jordan didn't bother explaining any of this. Judging from the look on your face, she neglected to mention him when she came running to you."

Ellie hated the seed of doubt Bethany was planting, with success even. She didn't want to believe any of it. It was true, Jordan wasn't fond of solving issues in conversation, but at some point, you had to trust a person. Bethany, as she was finding out, wasn't big on trust.

"You know, Jordan's parents were high school sweethearts—or at least, that's the first layer of the story, and quite a euphemism. They were too young when they got married, and by far not mature enough to care for a child. Drugs, alcohol, sleeping around, you get the picture. They didn't exactly provide a safe or stable home for her, and it's kind of a miracle she got to where she is now. There's a price to pay somewhere, always. It's hard to battle the genes."

"Really? Which genes are you battling?"

Bethany shook her head with a sad little patronizing smile. "I know you mean well, but please, don't get your hopes up too high. Jordan will come back to me, apologize, and that'll be it.

162

Believe me, we've been through this. Although, a guy? That's new."

"Look, Dr. Roberts, I'm sorry. I'm really sorry you got hurt in this, because I'm sure it wasn't Jordan's intention, and it sure as hell wasn't mine."

"This is not about me."

"If you say so."

Bethany left the car, slamming the door harder than necessary. By sheer force of will, Ellie held back tears.

❧

"I saw your girlfriend today," he said. She couldn't suppress the shudder. Jordan didn't want to think of Jonathan Darby and Ellie in the same room. No matter what she might still endure. "You know, I was always wondering, who might be the more important person to punish, the cheater, or the enabler. I might want to go back to her."

"No. Please, don't do that. She...it's not her fault. It's all mine."

Despite her demure manner, he hit her across the face. "I didn't ask for your opinion, did I? Of course it's your fault. That's what I'm trying to get through your thick skull."

"I know."

"I know what?" he mocked her. "You need to be a little clearer."

"I know you're trying. It's my fault. I want to learn, okay?" At least, Jordan hoped that was what he wanted to hear, and that it didn't sound as defensive as it had in her head.

"Sure you do." Within a heartbeat, his demeanor changed again, a smile spreading across his face. Jordan wasn't sure if it was a form of reassurance or a sign of worse things to come.

"Please leave Ellie alone. You have me now."

"Yeah, funny how it goes sometimes. Don't worry, I know what it's like with whores like you, they can't help themselves, but you can change. With a little education and..."

He held the object close to her face, making her cringe. "Oh, no, don't be scared. This will only hurry the process along. Don't fight it, and you'll be fine."

"Please, don't." The words were out of her mouth before she could stop them. The details from the autopsy reports and the hospital were too reminiscent on her mind. She was terrified of falling back into the memory of what had passed as a family party all those years back.

He pressed the plunger to rid the syringe of air bubbles, then pushed her sleeve aside. "The less you struggle, the less painful it will be. I told you, those are all the basics. It will get better once you made it through them. There, just a little prick."

She was fighting the loss of control, but the following warmth enveloping her was too tempting.

"I have high hopes for you, Jordan. Don't disappoint me." He stroked his hand along her thigh, and down her calf before he got up, looking down at her with an unreadable expression—or maybe she couldn't read it because her mind was unable to put together the clues.

He turned to leave once more.

❧

Ellie was in the same hyper-vigilant state she'd been in right after the attack. She had no choice but to do her job, as everyone else did, but in the past couple of days, she'd been unable to get more than a couple of hours of sleep. The nightmares were back full force. She might still be losing her mind as she'd feared around that time, but she wasn't going to buy into Bethany's theory.

As it seemed, Bethany had abandoned it too, looking more haggard and worried each time Ellie happened to run into her. The bank manager confirmed Jordan had been looking into the possibility of financing a house and started the process.

Jonathan Darby agreed to show the property to the investigators, though he claimed to have only met her there once. The owner had moved far away to Japan. Henderson didn't know it yet, but Ellie planned to invite herself to the viewing. She had found the maps. Maybe she'd be lucky again.

Meanwhile, no one really believed in Bethany's theory anymore, not even the profiler herself.

Detective Jordan Carpenter was officially missing. Ellie couldn't help thinking it could have been her.

Jordan had spent a big part of her childhood trying to keep a low profile so she wouldn't draw the attention of Child Protective Services and be taken away from her parents. Christina and Kevin, a couple who lived in the same trailer park and dropped in every now and then, had painted the likely future to her in ghastly colors. In a foster family, she wouldn't be the princess anymore, not like now. She'd be neglected, taken out of school, maybe even hit, that's what they told her.

Jordan didn't have much of a concept of what a princess was supposed to be, or why the term would be in any way correct to describe her circumstances. However, whenever she was hiding in the corner next to her bed, blocking out the loud voices and the laughter, she was wondering if a foster family would be at all different from the present. Sometimes, she was tempted to find out, but then she remembered she belonged with her parents, and they needed her. Who would help Mommy clean up after one of their parties, make sure there were meals on the table?

As she grew older, Jordan began to realize they needed her more than she needed them. She couldn't walk away, even if she could have seen any better alternatives.

That didn't mean she didn't hate it, the loud music, the clogging smell in the air, the clinking, and sometimes, breaking of a bottle.

"Isn't that the little princess?" Laughter. It echoed in her brain, made her head hurt. In an instant, she was violently sick, the painful spasm of her stomach lifting the veil of memory and drugs. Fortunately for Jordan, eventually someone had made sure she knew that she owed nothing to a couple of dysfunctional adults, even if they happened to be her birthparents. Kathryn and James Larson had given up their parental rights so Jordan could be adopted. In her opinion, it had been the only good thing they'd ever done for her, even if their actions made it painfully obvious they never wanted her to begin with.

She'd been able to start a new life. Whether or not she'd get another second chance to live wasn't so sure.

"Poor thing. I guess breakfast is out of the question?" The voice was mocking her, in the past, and the present. "Let's clean up here, and then we can continue for a bit before I go see the cops again. I'm going to show them your house, did I tell you that? Let's see how it goes over the next few days, and maybe you can even still move in. Wouldn't that be nice?"

He opened the cuffs.

It was only for a heartbeat Jordan entertained a possible escape because the moment she was on her feet, the ground seemed to disappear beneath her. She felt irrationally ashamed, thinking of Judy who had held out all this time. Only to have an incompetent cop mess up her rescue. She felt the tears hot on her face.

"It's okay," he said softly. "The bathroom is right over there."

Had she been in there before? How much time had passed?

The space behind the curtain wasn't much of a bathroom. There was a toilet, a sink, and a drain in the ground underneath a shower fixed to the wall. At least, he hadn't come in with her, so she hurried up ignoring the lack of privacy, struggling to clear her mind from the cobwebs. She spent a moment staring at her pitiful mirror image, trying to find any resemblance of hope and resolve when she needed most of it to stay upright.

Whatever drugs he had used on her were actually helping with the pain, but they also unleashed another kind of monster. The pain was preferable.

"Can you see it now? This is what a dirty whore looks like." He chuckled, his arrogant, entitled manner making her forget for a moment that she was facing a cold-blooded murderer, or that in her condition, she was no match for him.

"Damn it, Jordan," he hissed, pushing her back against the wall, his gloved fingers clamping down on her wrists. She wished she could have brought up her knee high enough to hit him where it hurt, but a futile attempt was all she could manage. "Don't you realize this is getting you nowhere? Do you want to start all over again?" He pressed down hard on the dirty bandage, and she went limp, to keep breathing, and not throwing up, the only incentive left.

"That's right, you need to stop fighting me and making it worse. Have you forgotten I know where Ellie lives?"

"Stay away from her."

"Or what?" He laughed.

"She's going to kick your ass." At this moment, Jordan was incredibly grateful for the officer still guarding Ellie's apartment. If Darby was really that bold, he was going to get caught. Soon. She was terrified of the alternatives.

"Oh yeah? We'll see about that." He let go of her abruptly but dropping her to the ground wasn't enough. When the blows started raining, she told herself she'd do whatever it took to keep him away from Ellie, but the hard truth was setting in as the shackles were back and she was held up by the cold unyielding chains once more. There wasn't much she could do to stop him from anything. He walked around her, regarding her, too damn pleased with himself.

"You know, I asked them to say it on video when I thought they were ready. Eleanor eventually did, but too bad, so sad, it was too late already. Isabel, she struggled a lot."

She was going to be sick again. She didn't want to hear this, any of it. So much pain. The memory. The present. The fear he could still want to go after Ellie.

"Why is it so hard to admit? I brought all the evidence, how you hurt other people, made their lives miserable, because you couldn't keep your legs together. They had punishments for that through the ages, and some of them looked a little like this. The Middle Ages are so underrated."

Jordan was fading in and out, as he ranted on about the merits of gruesome punishments in the course of history, but she flinched when he mentioned Bethany's name.

"You are failing her. You've done so for years, and the sooner you can admit I'm right, the better. Maybe you can see it, admit it, when temptation is gone." He stepped forward, unexpectedly close, and kissed her, hard. She sputtered.

"Maybe all you need is a little more convincing," Darby said.

Ellie did her best to keep her head down and blend in with the tasteful furniture. She was well aware Bethany was unhappy about her presence, and Derek would only tolerate it until the sergeant told him otherwise.

Jordan had bought a house on a whim, then disappeared. Ironically, Ellie could see her in these surroundings. The laid back, warm style seemed to fit her more than the modern apartment she shared with Bethany. Not that it was any of her concern at the moment, or that of the cops the realtor led through the house.

"I'm so sorry I can't help more," he said. "We came here only once. There would be no reason for her to come back without a key."

"Do you always seal a deal this quickly?" Henderson asked, skeptical.

"No, of course not, but when it's urgent, I try to get it done with as little hassle as possible. The owner was on a tight schedule, Jordan had the money, and she seemed desperate to move." He shrugged, hands in the pockets of his slacks. "Not that I know a lot about the circumstances. She just really wanted it to happen quickly."

Ellie caught Henderson's thoughtful look. *You don't know her well, yet you call her by her first name.*

Darby's agency and its team had a spotless record, yet half of the cases kept leading back to him. Bad luck?

"I hope nothing bad happened to her," he said. "I liked her, and I was happy to find a place that suited her needs so soon. Would that be all? I'm afraid I have other clients waiting as well."

Bethany turned on her heels and stalked away. For once, Ellie could sympathize with her.

The uncertainty was killing her too.

⁂

"No, no, no, that won't do it. You have to look at me."

No.

The slap made her teeth rattle, but it was almost better than the warm cocoon she was trapped in, slowly suffocating. She tried to hide, become invisible, but that never worked. They always saw her. The friends who came to her parents' parties were always friendly and in a good mood at first, but somehow, that never lasted.

"Listen to me. Concentrate."

Couldn't he see how hard she was trying? It wasn't enough. She could feel herself slip away. With difficulty, she raised her head.

"Now, that's better," he said, his voice gentle. "Let's continue, shall we?"

❦

"I need every available officer at the game tonight. That includes you, Harding." Sergeant Bristol's tone left no room for arguing. "We'll have to switch you back to nights too, for a couple of weeks. Don't," he held up a hand when she opened her mouth. "The detectives got it covered."

"Then why haven't they found her yet?"

"That's enough, Harding. Everyone is alert and on the lookout for her. Meanwhile those people deserve to enjoy the game safely."

There were many things Ellie wanted to say to that, like, why is there still an officer in front of my house when you think it's safe for me to be in that crowd? If it wasn't for that, the memory of the night she got attacked was still vivid on her mind, and she couldn't bear the thought that Jordan might suffer even worse at his hands.

For sure, life in the city didn't stop, though Ellie wished it would. Frankly, she couldn't care less about people wanting to enjoy a game, and she knew that attitude didn't make her useful for any kind of police work. She had to keep it together, find the missing piece. The sergeant's expression softened as he seemed to read her conflicting emotions in her expression.

"Take a couple of days off before you switch to nights," he advised. "I know this has been especially hard on you, but we'll find her. When we put away this perp, that'll give you some closure as well."

Ellie nodded, not convinced of anything he'd said. However, she had to take a step back, do her job. She might not empathize a lot with football fans today, but at least she shouldn't risk endangering anyone because her thoughts were elsewhere.

"Thanks, Sergeant. I hope so."

Working at the game was much of the usual, crowd control, breaking up drunken brawls, assisting the local security staff. Ellie was alternately bored out of her mind and ready to jump out of her skin, because she felt this meant wasting precious time. Of course, Derek wouldn't update her every hour, especially if there was no news, and Bethany didn't give a damn whether or not Ellie was in the loop.

Libby brought her a coffee, regarding her with so much sympathy Ellie felt uncomfortable.

"Look, I'm not sure I should say this, but it's pretty obvious you like her. I hope we'll find her soon."

"Yeah, me too," Ellie had to remind herself that snapping at her friend and colleague would not help anyone, least of all Jordan.

Back at the station, she noticed that neither Derek nor Bethany were in. The sergeant wasn't in his office either. Technically, she was off the clock, but she guessed no one would mind if she went over some of the papers once more...or copied them and brought them home.

For the first time since Rhonda had moved out, Ellie appreciated having all this space to herself. Within minutes, the coffee table and parts of the floor were littered with paper, grouped by subject. Lori Gleason's online acquaintances. The trophies they were aware of—coins and jewelry. The places that marked where the women had been held—and where bodies had been found. Had the killer taken something from Jordan's house, another trophy? Had he planned to take something from Ellie?

She sank to the floor, overwhelmed by the testimony of tragedy, all because one man thought he had the right to punish them, involving the naïve Gleason in his schemes. How petty was it to hire someone to harm a cheating spouse instead of divorcing them?

I'm so sorry, I'm trying. I want you to be safe.

With new resolve, she wiped her face and picked up the first pile. She'd go through each of the papers, each line, each letter, one by one. Something had to come up.

❧

"It's okay now. All done. I'm afraid I'll have to leave you for a bit now..." That got her attention as he knew it would. "I promise I'll be back soon. You did good."

Her lips moved, but she was too out of it to formulate the question. He knew what she meant to say though. "Don't worry. I'm not going to hurt her. I don't care about her anymore."

Now, how to get rid of the last person standing between him and his mission?

Chapter Fifteen

W hen Ellie woke up, the sun was shining through the
blinds. She felt slightly nauseated, and a headache was
pounding behind her temples. What the hell? She'd stayed up
way past midnight, but she hadn't had any alcohol. At least,
for the first time in forever, she'd slept so deeply she couldn't
remember any nightmares, but that didn't mean she felt rested.

It didn't matter.

She had to get up, get back to work, even though she'd do
it from home for the next couple of days. Ellie pushed back
the covers that seemed much heavier than before and swung
her feet over the edge of the bed, when the sensation registered
with her. She flashed back to taking a shower before going
to bed, putting on a shirt and—panties. She wasn't wearing
panties. Ellie frowned, trying to grasp a clear thought through
the headache, rising discomfort and fear. *Think, damn it.* There
had to be a rational explanation. Maybe she'd been too tired, had
just imagined she put them on, or was mixing it up with...no.
She did remember. She had put them on after the shower, the
same pair of black and pink lace Jordan had admired on her
what seemed forever ago.

If she hadn't taken them off—there was only one reason she
could think of, and the idea made her stomach churn. Ellie took
another pair out of her dresser and put them on, feeling better

instantly. When she opened the blinds, she saw the familiar car still sitting in its spot. She had to be imagining things. Nothing happened. Maybe she'd had an intense dream she didn't remember. No one had gotten past the cop in the car.

Except...

Her heart was racing so hard Ellie had trouble breathing when she saw the small object on the sheet. She picked up her phone and put it on speaker, dressing as she spoke to the 911 dispatcher.

"I'm coming with you. I'm fine!" she insisted, disregarding Henderson's quizzical look. "I'll do whatever you want me to do, but I need to see what's on this. I *need* to," Ellie stressed, hoping she could convince them without having a complete meltdown first. The cavalry had arrived. Judging from the cast of characters populating her living room, everybody was taking this very seriously.

"McCarthy, you go to the hospital with Harding," Henderson said, disregarding her protest altogether. "Ellie, if you don't remember anything, you have most likely been drugged. I want to make sure we check as long as the drug might still be in your system."

She blushed hotly, aware that a drug test wasn't the only thing he wanted her to go to the hospital for. At least she had cleaned up the papers sometime last night. It was a small comfort. Maybe there were some things she didn't want to know. Ellie had to know though what was on that USB key.

Kate touched her arm gently, and it took Ellie all the willpower she had left not to jump as high as the ceiling. "Come," she said. "I'll drive you to the department afterwards."

They drove in silence.

Ellie kept interactions, with her colleague, with the hospital staff, to a minimum, needing all her concentration to focus on the riddle.

"See, I think he's messing with us. I believe he lost interest in me the moment the little old lady called 911 on him. It's not me he wants, this is all for the message he wants to send. I'm sure he didn't hurt me." *That's because he already has the person he wants to hurt.*

The thought finally broke her composure. Kate pulled up on the parking lot of a grocery store, stopped the car and unfastened her seat belt. Then she wrapped her arms around Ellie.

The perpetrator they were looking for might target women in a specific situation, but at this moment, they shared the same anger and fear.

"We have to stop him," Ellie said.

Kate nodded grimly.

He was giving her choices, or pretending to do so, because you could never trust people like him. Jordan, in her more conscious moments, pretended to go along with his charade, gaining time, trying to think beyond fear or shame or the confusion caused by the drugs. If she survived this, if she was able to tell her story in a court, his days of freedom would be over. They'd be able to tie him to the murders and kidnappings without a doubt, even if Lori never remembered.

If only she hadn't been in so much pain, she might have found a way to get out of those shackles herself. Jordan knew there were many people motivated to find her, and they would. Eventually.

Before she could lose her mind trying to figure out how everything in her life had gone so horribly wrong, and if there was still the sliver of a chance for her to get it right, maybe even with someone who could love and respect her.

Jordan didn't doubt for a moment that Ellie was brave enough to try. The memory of her embrace was the only thing safe. That had to mean something.

Of course, he would try to spoil that for her too.

"You've been taking some important steps, Jordan," he told her when he returned. "I brought you a present."

She only caught a quick glimpse at the fabric he threw at her, but Jordan recognized the garment, her worst fears confirmed in an instant. It didn't matter how far she was willing to go to divert his attention, he wasn't going to humor her.

Which meant she couldn't wait, hoping someone would find her, because this wasn't just about her. He had targeted both Lori and Isabel, and apparently, he was planning the same once more.

"Tell me what you did to her," she said. *...and make no mistake, you'll pay for it.*

He gave her a long, considering look. "Oh, I didn't do anything to her. The problem with Isabel was that she couldn't make up her mind, so I had to try and educate both her and Lori. You or Ellie—you've been very specific. I stand by my promise. I choose you." He smiled, and Jordan knew she'd have to retreat deeply into her mind. It was the only way.

<hr />

"I'm not going home. I did everything you asked me to do, now I want to see it."

"It's none of your Goddamn business!" Bethany yelled at her. Her eyes were rimmed with red. "For Christ's sake, when are you going to take a hint?"

"Dr. Roberts." Bristol's voice had a warning tone to it, which she ignored.

"Why is she even still here?"

"*She* is currently having her locks changed," Ellie muttered. "I'll stay with Kate for a couple of days until everything is settled."

"My concern is for Jordan's safety and her privacy," Bethany insisted. "I don't want any more people to see this video than is absolutely necessary. How could Officer Harding possibly help us? She was asleep when he delivered the key!"

"That's enough. There was a sedative in her bloodstream, as you know. Officer Harding remains an important witness. This isn't easy to watch," he addressed Ellie, "but if there's anything that might jog your memory, anything that could help, I'll take the risk. I believe privacy is the last of our worries, or Detective Carpenter's, at this point. I want this guy."

"I'll be down in the lab," Derek said, "see if they found anything."

"All right then. I come with you. Let's see if we can 'jog' anything."

It took Ellie a moment to realize Bethany had spoken to her.

❧

The screen brought a nightmare to life, Jordan, scarcely dressed, her gaze unfocused, the discoloration on the side of her face standing out against the paleness of her skin.

"Oh my God." Ellie didn't realize she'd said it out loud, until Bethany chastised her.

"Keep it together. You wanted to see it."

She stayed silent after that, though the high-pitched voice that followed made her jump.

"Listen to me. Concentrate."

Ellie had never felt so useless in all her life.

"Now, that's better. Let's continue, shall we?" The fact that he went to the length distorting his voice to this cadence of deranged cartoon character showed he was worried about being recognized. Would she be able to identify his voice? Ellie doubted it. Useless. They had to wait for the lab tech's analysis, and that would take some time. She knew exactly how Jordan had felt about the urgency of Judy Lawrence's case, but this was worse, much worse.

"Okay." Jordan's voice was strained, slightly slurred as if the drugs and pain were warring in her system. However, she managed to look at the camera this time. "First of all...Beth, I'm so sorry. I didn't mean to hurt you, but it's all true. I cheated on you...not the first time, and I know I deserve this."

Ellie could only stare in disbelief.

"I'm a whore. I deserve to die. I'll do better, I promise."

The video faded to black, leaving her and Bethany in a heavy, pregnant silence.

Finally, Bethany got up to click 'play again'. "Just in case you remember something," she said.

Ellie ignored the sarcasm, thinking when she picked up some clothes to go to Kate's, she'd have to bring the printouts. Go over them again.

Beth, I'm so sorry.

I cheated on you. I deserve to die.

Beth.

"How many times do you think you can stand to see this? Are you going to find something that no one else did? Let's give it a try."

"Dr. Roberts, please."

"Come on, I thought you were this division's rising star, and since you're such an expert on Jordan too, go ahead, solve the case."

Bethany was just as terrified, Ellie realized. What was she missing?

Kate was meeting Jensen tonight, so Ellie had plenty of time to resume her search for the needle in the haystack. She was exhausted, overcaffeinated and trying to ignore that the same man who had filmed Jordan, had also broken into Ellie's apartment, drugged her and stolen a rather intimate piece of clothing. It was all too much to think about, yet she pored over the same documents, some of which Jordan had asked her to read on her first day with the task force.

Lori had had interesting exchanges with men and women, besides Gordon Chambers, a date to which she'd never shown up. She'd teamed up with Bella a.k.a. Isabel to go looking for a third party at the All Colors. Somebody had found them, somebody with a vengeance of their own.

Bethany had been to Seattle, looking into the case of Chantal Perron, but she hadn't told Jordan until she was officially assigned to the task force. Why?

Why had Bethany alleged Jordan could have just disappeared on her own, when she knew the stakes of this case? For the umpteenth time, Ellie went over the printouts of Lori Gleason's emails and chats.

There were the contents of her husband's computer. He had been slightly more careful, but there were a handful of emails that appeared to be relevant, sender unknown. The account had already been deleted by the time the police got their hands on this data, and digging deeper took time.

"I tried to message you, why don't you answer? They found out about Seattle."

"*Don't worry about Seattle,*" the punisher had answered. "*I have a friend who will look into this for a favor.*"

It always came back to the same people. Maybe that's where she had to take a closer look.

It was over. She'd lost. Judy had probably died the day she'd arrived here, and in spite of all his phony promises, he was still watching Ellie. There was nothing she could do. Jordan vaguely remembered the camera, her own stumbling words, the memory making her cringe. She had managed to uphold a certain appearance to everyone in her life except Bethany—and maybe Ellie.

Not because she poked and prodded, but because she was willing to take a closer look at things most people liked to gloss over. Maybe they could have worked out in the long run, if it wasn't for the man who'd seen right through all of Jordan's insecurities.

What he'd made her say on the video was so ridiculous, but thinking of it didn't make her laugh, on the contrary. This was how they'd remember her. The realization, oddly, hurt more than any of the physical pain he'd inflicted on her.

Chapter Sixteen

"You can't stay away, can you?" It was more frustration than anything in Henderson's voice, Ellie decided, and she knew this frustration wasn't directed at her. She wondered whether she should share her suspicion with him. Could it harm? He had worked with Jordan for many years. If there was any, albeit small chance they could save her, he'd listen.

"How well do you know Dr. Roberts?" Testing the waters.

He groaned. "Not now, Ellie. She might not be the warmest person I know, but she knows her job and that is all I care about. There'll be time to sort out everything else once we find Jordan, don't you think?"

"I didn't mean—"

"You're worried, and exhausted, I get that. We all are. Unlike us, you have the luxury of going home, so I suggest you do that."

"I will. Just one more thing. Do you trust her?"

"Her resumé speaks for itself. I'm sorry, Ellie, I've got to go."

Ellie didn't question any of Bethany's credits, but her position was also a good one to hide behind. After Derek had left, she made sure no one was watching her, and then sat behind the computer Bethany had used earlier. She knew she was desperate. If Bethany was in any way involved, she'd be better at covering her tracks than that, but Ellie had to try. She opened a drawer to find a flyer for a medieval market, and a business card from the realtor, Jonathan Darby.

Was he the man Sheila's colleague at the All Colors had seen talking to Lori and Bella? Had anyone ever followed up on that? Now was a moment as good as any.

Sheila was working behind the counter when Ellie arrived. Obviously, she wasn't happy to see Ellie again after barely escaping with her life and coming close to losing her job. She had fully cooperated with the police, so the All Colors wouldn't be closed down altogether, and she could continue to work here.

"What now?"

"I won't bother you for long," Ellie promised, thinking the woman could be a little more grateful considering the police had saved her life as well. "Can you just tell me if you ever saw him?" She had printed out a picture of Darby from his website.

Sheila's sullen expression turned to surprise. "I saw him only once, but I'm pretty sure he hung out with Bella and Lori that night. They got into a fight over something, and he left. It wasn't when either of them disappeared though. Wait...I think he had drinks with Lori's husband once. I could be mistaken though." That was, well, a little better than nothing. She'd found a picture of Bethany as well, from a newspaper article, but Sheila shook her head. "I would have remembered her."

Ellie suppressed a sigh. "Thank you so much. This helps a lot."

Her next stop was at Lori Gleason's. She was lucky the woman knew her, because otherwise she might not have opened the door to Ellie, especially since she wasn't in uniform.

"Are you all right?"

Those were not the first words she had expected from a woman who'd barely escaped a serial killer. Ellie cast a self-conscious look at herself in the mirror next to the wardrobe. She looked a bit frantic. What was she to do when everyone seemed to believe she was imagining things, and they weren't looking for Jordan in the right place? Was she looking in the right place?

Lori had to help her, because there was something that bound them together now, her, Jordan, and Lori. They had to end it, if they ever wanted to be free from the boundaries one man had inflicted on them, because he felt he had the right to do so.

"I am fine," she said, trying not to sound irritated. "I just need you to answer me one question. Do you know this man?"

Lori looked puzzled when Ellie showed her the picture. "The other cops already asked me. Mr. Darby worked with my husband a few times, and he sold the house where..." She swallowed hard. "...where the cops found me that day."

"Yes, I know, but did you ever talk to him in any other context?"

Lori shook her head.

"Someone told me they saw you with him and Bella, at the All Colors. Please, Lori, this is important."

"They must be mistaken," Lori insisted. "There's nothing I can tell you."

Something about her choice of words struck Ellie as odd. Then again, they were both at the end of their line. Odd had become the usual.

"I'd like to leave this picture with you, and here's my private cell phone number. If you remember anything, please call me, day or night."

Lori accepted the picture and card but turned away almost immediately.

"Please leave."

"I will. Remember, he can't hurt you anymore."

"He's still out there." Lori laughed bitterly. "Unless you kill the monsters, don't they always come back?"

Ellie didn't have an answer for her.

She left a message with Kate, just to be on the safe side, before she made the drive to Darby's estate, an impressive Victorian-style building. She wasn't an expert, but there were elements Ellie thought looked Gothic. There was his possible connection to Judy Lawrence.

It was obvious to her that Lori hadn't told the truth. Was he still threatening her? What was his endgame? Was it always the kill, did he mean to draw it out, or did he simply enjoy knowing there were women living in fear he might come back for them?

<hr />

Judy vaguely remembered making it out the front door of the house of horrors, almost falling down the stairs, catching herself again. Stumbling across the front yard, down the driveway. She knew it was important to find a house, get help, but the old barn was as far as she made it. Now, for the first time, she was awake for longer than a few minutes, more aware of her surroundings.

Judy wanted to hide out in the barn forever, never again see or speak to another person, but she was so hungry, and there was still the other woman with him. Lori...No, he had moved Lori. The woman had said she was with the police.

Judy was terrified that he could still come after her, a fear that was choking her, rendering her paralyzed. She had to move. Get away. There had to be people in the house, a phone. She would break a window if she had to.

She still couldn't understand what had happened to her, or why, but she felt the urgency. Someone had come for her, and that woman was in mortal danger.

"Ma'am?"

She flinched violently at the male voice, her eyes darting around wildly, looking for an escape. The man who had found her wasn't her tormentor. In fact, as he raised his flashlight, she could see the shocked expression in his face.

"Peggy!" he shouted. "Come on over here, quick!"

"Please, don't hurt me. Don't hurt me," Judy whimpered, sinking to her knees.

"What happened?" The woman arrived behind her husband.

Judy crumbled to the floor, holding her head in her hands. "Please, no." They were going to punish her, for sure. No one tolerated an intruder, be it in one's home, or relationship.

"I think we should call the police," the woman said, her voice shaky.

"No kidding, and an ambulance too," the husband agreed. "It looks like she's hurt."

"Don't you see?" Peggy interrupted him. "This is the woman the police are looking for, Judy Lawrence. She was on the news, remember?"

Judy hoped she had paid her dues because she couldn't cling to consciousness any longer.

❧

"I know you said the words, but did you mean them? Have you accepted your punishment?"

He touched the side of her face lightly. Jordan cringed, not from pain, but the way her mind went crazy whenever he touched her like this, infecting her with the fear of what might happen. Memory. Reality. It was clear to her that he had done a lot of homework on all his victims, otherwise he couldn't know about the trailer, or all those other little details of her history he liked to throw back into her face.

This wasn't her, not anymore. As long as she was conscious, she had to hold on to the image of a woman who had been fairly competent on the job, and just getting used to the notion she might be lovable.

"I have." Pretense, lie, truth?

"Good. Then we can move on to the next stage."

He went to the bathroom and, moments later, returned with a large bucket. Jordan had only split seconds to wonder about his intention before he poured the ice-cold water over her. She gasped, trying to catch her breath against the harsh sensation.

Darby looked down at her, his gaze impassive. "A whore who's sorry is still a dirty whore, you know? Don't worry though. We're getting there. Sooner than you think." He leaned down to brush the wet hair out of her face. She was shaking hard, her body reacting to the overload of fatigue and pain.

"In fact, I think we could start the last phase right now. With Judy sneaking away and your little girlfriend putting things together, we have a little less time now."

It was funny how he called Ellie her girlfriend, when he had made her beg Bethany for forgiveness. Also...Judy had gotten away. Maybe she had survived.

"You think we need those?" he asked, brushing a finger over the shackles. "Will you be good if I open them?"

She could tell this would be the deciding moment, and she could increase her chances in degrees if she made the right decision—or maybe she had already become delusional and there was no chance she could defeat him, with or without shackles. She had to try, for herself, and all the other women.

"I'll do what you say."

His smile was smug as he looked her up and down. "Yes, you will," he whispered.

Jordan was uncomfortably aware of how the fabric, once crisp white, stuck to her skin. Her hands shook so badly he probably thought it was safe to let her out of the shackles—he wanted her to struggle a bit at least.

She was going to give him all the fight she had left in her.

The shackles finally fell, and Jordan had a moment of irrational regret thinking the marks they left would scar.

"You're all mine now, Jordan. It's time."

"No, it's *your* time now. Get away from her."

He froze, and so did Jordan. Neither of them had expected to hear Ellie's voice in here.

⁂

It wasn't until she returned to her home and received a text message from a friend that Kate McCarthy got to check her voicemail and found Ellie's urgent sounding message. As she listened, her gaze fell on the papers Ellie had left lying on the kitchen table, all of them copies relating to the serial killer case and the disappearance of Detective Carpenter.

Since they'd come back from clubbing, where both she and Jensen had a few drinks, they couldn't go and check it out. She was worried and feeling guilty for finding the message so late.

She'd take the chance and check if Henderson was still at the station. He might know more.

"Are you sure you have to do this tonight?" Jensen asked. "Ellie is already in over her head."

"That's exactly what I'm worried about. Let's take a cab. Could you call? I'll try to get Henderson in the meantime."

"Sure, I'll—wow, take a look at this," he said, pointing at the screen of the TV he'd switched on when they came in.

The local channel was reporting Breaking News, movement in the disturbing serial killer case. The latest victim, Judy Lawrence, had been found alive in a farmer's barn.

"Wait." Kate picked up the papers once more. The copies were chat and email transcripts, and from the maps they had found in Gleason's house. Ellie had marked a point in the center of one map, the home address of realtor Jonathan Darby she'd wanted to check out tonight. It was less than a mile away from where Judy Lawrence had turned up.

Chapter Seventeen

"What is this?" Jonathan Darby asked, sounding amused. "Are you jealous I changed my mind? Why, I'm so sorry, Ellie. I guess I prefer brunettes after all."

"Turn around, slowly, with your hands where I can see them."

"Come on, you're smarter than that, aren't you? You didn't think I'd let you come down here if I didn't know how to deal with intruders?"

Ellie looked around and decided he was messing with her. The trap door didn't magically close, and there was nothing suggesting an imminent threat. She avoided the falling chains at the last moment, but hit her shoulder on the concrete floor, the gun slipping from her fingers.

Not now, damn it. She couldn't afford to lose the vague sense of safety the cold steel in her hands had presented or slip into a flashback of that night she walked home from the bar. As she struggled to her feet, he gripped the chain, advancing on her.

"I like those," he said. "Really solid, you can break bones with them. Do you still have nightmares, Ellie? Do you remember our night?"

She backed up a step, wondering if Kate had found the message and drawn her conclusions from it. In any case, she didn't have a lot more time. She needed to get Jordan and herself out of this hell.

When he raised the chains, she ducked, trying to break the impact with her hands, trying to get a hold of them. She might be tired, but being so close to ending the ongoing nightmare, gave her a jolt of adrenaline. She managed to grip one end and launch it into his face.

Ellie might not have broken any bones, but the blood spurting from his nose was a satisfying sight.

"Not...anymore." She meant to step aside but slipped in what she recognized too late as a puddle. He was coming at her again, and then a shot rang out, and Darby dropped to the ground with a surprised look on his face. He was unconscious, but to be safe, Ellie wrapped some of the heavy chains around his ankles. She'd have to keep an eye on him until help arrived.

She finally dared to look at Jordan who had lowered the gun but held on to it in a white-knuckled grip. Ellie would have done the same if their roles were reversed.

"Thank you," she said softly. "You can give it to me now. I can take it from here." In fact, she didn't think Jordan could take any more. Their hands touched briefly when she handed Ellie the gun. Jordan's were ice-cold, trembling, which wasn't a surprise, given her state of dress, a tattered shirt over bra and panties. She was drenched in cold water.

"It's over," Ellie said, needing to convince both of them. She couldn't let her imagination and fears run wild now. "I left a message with Kate. She knows I'm here."

Jordan mustered a wry smile. "Smarter than I was. Don't...turn your back to him."

Ellie cast a quick glance towards Darby, who didn't move.

"I won't." She shrugged out of her cardigan and put it around Jordan's shoulders, carefully, trying to avoid causing her any more pain. If she could get to her feet, maybe they could make it up those stairs? She could call for more backup, and she'd feel better once they could lock him in down here. That was the priority. Everything else could wait.

"Let's get out of here. Come. Let me..." She holstered her gun, offering both hands to help her up. Jordan went with the movement, but she paled, and her eyes welled up.

"I know. Just a little bit longer. You made it this far. I know you're hurt. We'll go slow. Help is on the way."

She was afraid she was going to lose her if they didn't move now. On the floor, Darby groaned, trying to get the heavy chains off him. Ellie stayed behind Jordan, carefully watching her, the slow pace heartbreaking. "I'm sorry," she whispered. Two, three steps, it seemed to take forever.

Then, finally, voices, noise from above.

"We're here!" she shouted, then remembering the room she'd come through was soundproof. She had found this place, so would they, right?

Ellie froze when a hand clamped around her ankle and pulled sharply. She tried to hold on to something, but there was no railing, and her hands flailed in mid-air.

"Go!" she yelled before she lost her footing and tumbled back into darkness.

⁂

Jonathan Darby had not counted in how angry she was, for the sense of safety he'd robbed her of, the nightmares, the other women he'd hurt, including the one she...No, now wasn't a good time to analyze her feelings for Jordan. Ellie was back on her feet instantly, lashing out and kicking. Fortunately, the gunshot had slowed down Darby.

"Ellie! It's okay. You're okay. You've got him."

The concerned face of Derek Henderson came into view. Taking a deep breath, Ellie stepped back, staggering.

"You'll be next!" Darby hissed. "Don't think you can escape your punishment!"

Ellie was tempted to kick him again, but she wouldn't have given in to the impulse even if it wasn't for Derek's hand on her shoulder. She knew Darby would use every possible, no matter how ridiculous, chance of accusing her if that meant he could slither out of some of the charges.

"Do you know how we *punish* murdering bastards? We put their asses in jail."

"That's right," Derek said. "The ambulance is waiting outside. Let's get upstairs."

"Hey, honey, you were waiting for me?" Darby sneered at Jordan.

They had gone much too easy on him, Ellie thought bitterly when, at the sight of Jordan, he seemed to forget all about his injuries. Bethany was with her. She had discarded Ellie's cardigan in favor of a blanket.

"Jordan, you must know you were my favorite," Darby yelled when the uniformed cops lead him to the squad car. "I enjoyed teaching you most of all." He laughed, a crazy eerie sound that made Ellie want to punch him, but instead she directed her attention at Jordan. She looked lost, even with her girlfriend's arm around her. Ellie moved her shoulder, wincing at the sharp pain she hadn't felt earlier when he pulled her back down into the basement. Now, it made itself known with a vengeance.

She made a step forward, only to have Bethany cast her a warning glance.

"Ellie! Thank God! I'm so glad you're all right!" Kate pulled her into a brief embrace.

"Ouch."

"Sorry. I sent backup right when I saw your message, because, get this, they found Judy too, and she's alive! This is a good day, even though you're going to hear from the sergeant for coming here by yourself."

"I did call for backup," Ellie said, irritated. "I called you."

Jordan would be happy to hear about Lawrence, though at the moment, she didn't seem much aware of her surroundings.

All that mattered was that they had made it through. Everything else would come together, as long as they both still believed they had a chance.

❦

"I'm fine!"

"No, you're not. We are not fine." As usual, Bethany saw right through her, which Jordan found even more unnerving at the moment. She was as far from fine as a person possibly could be, about to jump out of her skin, and Bethany holding her hands tightly didn't help. She wanted to escape, and she might have if she hadn't been so damn tired. Bethany knew that about her too.

She had refused medication to help her sleep, for the fear of waking up half naked and in chains. Her chest tightened painfully. How long ago? She hadn't managed to establish a timeline yet. All she knew was she had been well on the verge of going crazy, might have toppled over it if it wasn't for the thought of Ellie. Ironic that it was Ellie who had saved her, but Bethany was here with her instead. She was right. They were not fine. The tears came against her will, anger, only making her cry harder.

"I bet you have a suggestion."

Bethany picked up the box of tissues from the nightstand and held it out to her.

"Actually, I do, but there's time. First of all, we have to fix you up a bit. We can talk about it at home."

That reminded her of something. "Beth...I bought a house." Jordan froze, only now remembering the camera, her words. Was that real or just another drug-induced nightmare?

"Well, I'm sure we can do something about that. You don't have to worry about anything now. I'll take care of everything, okay?"

"It's my house. I can afford it, and I want to keep it."

"It was also sold to you by a monster, remember?" Bethany laughed a little. "It can't be that bad living with me. You were not thinking clearly."

"I want that house."

"Okay then. I'm not going to fight with you today of all days. I'm so relieved we found you."

"Ellie did." Jordan wasn't sure why she had to insist at this particular moment. Bethany frowned. "Sure, and she almost got herself killed in the process. Didn't anyone teach the girl procedure? Calling a friend who's off duty and clubbing with the boyfriend, doesn't quite count, even if they're cops. Those rookies." She shook her head, amused. "Next year, she wants to be a detective."

I wouldn't be here if it wasn't for her, Jordan thought, but she sensed there was no point in sharing this assessment with Bethany.

"I want to sleep." Her voice was dangerously shaky again. "Can we talk tomorrow?" Surely she deserved a small timeout before facing more hard questions.

"Of course," Bethany said, brushing her hand over Jordan's hair. "You should rest now. I'll stay here."

"No...You can go home. Tomorrow's going to be a long day."

"Yes, but..."

"Beth, please. I'd like to be by myself for a bit." In fact, it was rapidly becoming urgent. It wasn't Bethany's fault she kept reminding Jordan of everything that had gone wrong, between them, and what had put her on Darby's radar as a suitable subject. She'd have to face reality soon enough. For tonight, she wanted to pretend there was another way, another life.

"Okay. Sure." Bethany stood, unsure. "Can you reach the button? Are you in pain?"

"I'm fine," Jordan said once more, going with the trusted familiar pattern. They both knew which of them the liar was.

❦

Ellie had been stalling. Even though there was nowhere she'd rather be at the moment than with Jordan, she had joined her colleagues at the department, given her statement, listened to the sergeant's lecture she knew she deserved.

"Harding, I don't even know where to start."

Ellie realized she had to be close to being delirious, because she had the urge to laugh at his words. "Neither do I, sir."

She had to be careful. Neither a giggling nor a crying fit would make her look good now.

"You understand there have to be consequences. We teach you the rules for a reason."

"I know. I'm sorry. It's just that—" Blaming Bethany's attitude towards her wouldn't help, so Ellie held back the words that had been on the tip of her tongue. "Never mind. I know I should have requested backup officially."

"Yes, you should have."

"I was afraid of looking silly," Ellie confessed. "Detective Henderson and Dr. Roberts were busy."

"Let's hope we're not all looking silly once Darby goes to trial, because his lawyer will want to exploit every possible weakness in the case."

"He hurt her! You didn't see—" Again, she stopped herself, aware they had caught the attention of some officers outside Bristol's office. "No defense attorney can argue that away. We can tie him to the murders, and the abduction of Judy Lawrence and Lori Gleason too."

"Which is a good thing," he agreed. "We're all grateful this has come to an end. You know I can't overlook you neglecting procedure, but...Detective Carpenter owes you her life. You were brave down there."

"Thanks," Ellie murmured.

"By the way, this time when I tell you to take a few days off, you'll do it. Frankly you look horrible."

"Thank you, sir."

"Now go home. Sleep. Believe me, you need it."

It was hard to argue with that, but she'd stop by the hospital anyway. Leaving the office, she nearly ran into Kate who stepped inside, her expression serious.

"Sergeant? I thought you should see this right away."

Chapter Eighteen

E llie would have done anything to watch as Dr. Bethany Roberts had to explain herself for the messages exchanged with Jonathan Darby, the man who'd planned to murder her girlfriend as punishment for cheating on her.

As it was, nobody had the time or incentive to stop Ellie and so she stood, her jaw dropping with each secret uncovered.

"Yes, I was trying to bait him," Bethany said. "I didn't know who he was, I didn't manage to trace him, but I figured he would reveal himself at some point, want to meet me. I wish he'd have done that before going after Jordan, but I had to try. There were many lives at stake."

Ellie's suspicions had been right—partly at least. There had been some communication between Darby and Bethany, even though she hadn't known that the realtor was the killer she'd been chatting with.

"I never heard his voice before, that's why I couldn't tell." There was something haunted in her expression. "You know as well as I do this case wasn't moving along fast enough, and we had to do something. I kept in touch with my supervisor through all of it."

"Well, it's good to know you kept someone in the loop at least." Bristol's tone was dripping with sarcasm. "The next time you put the life of one of our detectives on the line, tell *me* first.

Well, if there's a next time, because I'll let your supervisor know I'm not happy with your conduct."

"The case is closed, isn't it?" Bethany said icily. "We drew him out. I know his type. I've helped put away a few of them. You can ask Detective Carpenter about the cases we worked together."

"I don't believe this," Bristol said angrily.

"Well, why am I in here and not your rookie, while we're talking transgressions and creative investigation methods?"

Ellie turned away, knowing if she listened a minute longer, a meltdown would be inevitable. She preferred to have it at home. Now that Jonathan Darby was in custody, she'd be safe there after all.

Jordan had been sleeping when she arrived at the hospital. Ellie didn't want to disturb her, so she finally went home, took a long hot shower, and collapsed on her bed. She didn't even have time to think or cry, sleep overtaking her almost immediately. She slept through the alarm a few hours later, and the sounds of the city beginning another busy morning. It was close to 11:00 a.m. when consciousness returned, with a wave of dizziness and nausea, as recollection set in. Ellie waited it out before she shuffled into the bathroom.

She decided to get a coffee on the way.

If she was lucky, she could talk to Jordan without Bethany's interference. If not now, soon.

Ellie stopped at a coffee shop, sitting in the parking lot with her latte for a few minutes, watching people go in and out. With all the buzz and chatter going on, it seemed unreal to think of the horrors that had taken place in the home of Jonathan Darby, deranged fan of medieval torture methods. The video. The chains. This was the fate she'd escaped, more than once.

Jordan had been lucky, but not that lucky. Ellie was determined to put her own pain aside for the moment. They might not have started out under the best circumstances, but whatever it was between them, it was real. It would help them both survive.

Much to their credit, neither Derek nor the sergeant treated her like she was about to break, in the hospital, and later, when she was back at the apartment, on sick leave. Jordan was incredibly grateful. The sympathy, the unspoken questions of the people around her felt stifling enough, especially when she couldn't move into her own space yet. She might never have all the answers because part of the time she'd spent in the hidden basement was lost in a haze of drugs. She was slowly gaining back control over her body though the urge to throw up at random memories was still strong. It would vanish at some point like the constant ache, all over, from the unnatural strain caused by the chains holding her up.

She shuddered, and predictably, Bethany was by her side with a concerned expression, ready to offer a glass of water, a blanket, or just about anything Jordan would ask of her.

None of this was Bethany's fault. She was trying hard, like she always did, and probably still feeling guilty.

Once her own mind was a bit less fuzzy, Jordan would find the moment to tell her she'd probably been on Darby's list early on. Bethany's interference had offered him another opportunity to mess with them, trick them into a game of guilt and shame.

Then again, when had it started in the first place?

"I made an appointment," Bethany said. "Next Monday."

They'd agreed on a compromise. Bethany's contribution was for Jordan to keep the house. She thought it would be a good idea to have an investment property, something they could rent out soon. Jordan had no intention to rent it out.

"Excuse me for a moment."

"Sure." Bethany nodded with a pained look. She knew exactly what Jordan was going to do.

She picked up the cordless phone on the way to the bedroom. Ellie picked up mid-second ring.

"Ellie."

"Hey. I'm glad you called. I was told to leave you alone, so...I'm sorry."

There was no doubt as to who had told her that. Jordan was surprised and a bit disappointed Ellie had complied. She took a deep breath. It was good to hear Ellie's voice, a bit of warmth breaking through the ever-present chill. She might not be entirely fair to Bethany, but it was the way she felt.

"It's okay. You needed some time for yourself too," Jordan acknowledged. An expectant pause followed. "We need to talk. In person." 'Need' had a multitude of connotations right now.

"I'd love to, but how are we going to do that?" Ellie sounded uncertain.

"Are you home?"

"What about Bethany?" Ellie asked.

It was on the tip of her tongue to say she'd never cared before, but Jordan was well aware neither Ellie nor Bethany deserved her anger and short temper. *Yeah, what about Bethany?*

"Should you even drive?"

"I'll take a cab," Jordan said. "Wait for me?"

❦

Ellie had been waiting nervously. She still had many questions, but the quest for answers lost all meaning when Jordan walked into her home, still looking worse for wear though the visible signs of her ordeal were fading. Ellie knew too well that others would linger.

She wanted to hug her close, but didn't dare to, for several reasons.

"Come on in," she said unnecessarily. "Sit."

"Thanks."

They shared a brief, hesitant kiss before sitting on opposite ends of the couch. Ellie couldn't help thinking of the last time they'd been together, before the horror started. Making out in a public restroom. Sleeping in each other's arms because Jordan had decided she wanted to be with her. Ellie felt her throat go tight. Not yet. She needed to keep it together for this conversation. Given what Jordan had been through, Ellie's worries were not priority at the moment.

"So...what are you going to do with the house?"

"I bought it. It's mine," Jordan said, and Ellie's heart missed a beat. There were many ways they could go from here. It didn't mean they were moving in together anytime soon, but it was a step forward.

"He handled many sales, and strangely enough, his business was all legit, not one missed document. There's no reason why you shouldn't keep it."

"That's what I thought. Ellie..."

She dared to move a bit closer. "Don't worry. I know we can't hit a switch and go back to the way it was before, but I am here for you, no matter how much time you need."

"Ellie, what I came to tell you..." Jordan was wringing her hands in her lap, avoiding Ellie's gaze.

Ellie couldn't stop looking at her bandaged wrists. "Whatever it is, we'll be okay."

"I can't...Bethany got us a therapist who does couples' counseling. I agreed to meet him."

"What? I thought...Why?"

"I know, it sounds crazy, but maybe I can actually learn some-thing. I wonder what Darby would have to say about this."

He'd made her apologize to Bethany. Ellie could only imagine what threats he'd had hanging over Jordan the whole time.

"I don't understand," she said. "I mean, besides..." *Us.* "You said you'd leave her, and if I remember correctly, you had some good reasons." She wanted to keep her tone calm and support-ive. The last thing Jordan needed was jealousy and accusations. However, Ellie needed to understand, and she was sure Jordan would see as well that she was about to make a big mistake.

"I changed my mind. I've been running from the truth for so long...I guess this is the end of the line. I can't run anymore."

She got to her feet. Ellie followed her.

"Jordan, please don't do this. She doesn't love you."

"I know...but I owe her."

It was Jordan who wrapped her arms around her, tightly enough to make them both wince.

"Why?"

"There was this one time...I wanted to kill myself."

A blurry veil descended over Ellie's vision. She closed her eyes, unwilling to let go.

"It was a particular bad time, and for some reason it all came floating to the surface again, reminding me. If she hadn't been there for me at the time...I don't know. I owe her to give this one last try."

Ellie thought of what Bethany had told her about Jordan's family, realizing that until now, she'd hoped it would be nothing but lies. No matter how much she disliked Bethany, the woman was a respected professional. She wasn't a liar simply because Ellie resented her.

"She can't hold that over you forever."

"She doesn't. I do." Jordan hesitated for a few heartbeats before she continued, "Thinking of you was the only thing that kept me sane down in that room—but I can't keep you waiting forever just because it might not work out in the end."

"I would." Ellie refrained from pointing out the relationship between Jordan and Bethany was more than likely not to work out, and why not spare everyone the resulting pain of a futile attempt? She couldn't make that decision for Jordan though. Only Jordan could.

"Don't." Jordan kissed her on the lips, very gently. "I want you to know I'm grateful, for everything. I don't want to drag you into this mess anymore. You'll do better. I'll see you around."

Ellie wanted to hold her back, but she was too dispirited to do so.

⌘

Bethany had taken some time off as well, attentive and caring every moment of the day though she refused to mention Jordan's visit to Ellie at all. The sad thing was Jordan didn't mind seeing the shrink, in fact, she knew she needed one to help her figure out if she could ever escape the traps laid out in her childhood, snapping shut one by one over the years. Bethany had once saved her from the ghosts of her past, even though these days, she was enabling them.

Jordan wanted to get away from her too, but apparently there was no point in trying, so she'd settle for trying to get well enough to go back to work. Maybe when she did, and Bethany returned to headquarters, she wouldn't feel like suffocating anymore.

"I'm doing better," she told him. "I think I'll be able to go back to work in a week, at the latest."

"You woke up crying again last night," Bethany said, and Jordan shot her an irritated glance.

"So? It wasn't fun spending those days half-naked in a killer's basement, wondering what he'd come up with next. It doesn't mean I can't work."

"I didn't say that. I just think it's too early."

Jordan caught the psychiatrist watching their interaction. "Right. That's pretty much representative of our communication."

"Jordan," Bethany chided.

"Why, it's true."

"I know you went through something terrible, but could you try not being difficult?"

"Bethany, how do you think Jordan feels about being called difficult?" the psychiatrist asked.

Bethany scoffed, his method obviously not her preferred one.

⌒⌒

The unintended humor was lost on her when she sat in the car later, struggling to shake the feeling of being naked and helpless once more. Not that the shrink had gone all the way yet, in fact, he was going fairly easy on her. The additional pressure of the pretense weighed on Jordan as well.

She had bought a house she might not ever live in. She wasn't with the person she longed to be with, even though Jordan had to admit she might have no idea what a sane, healthy relationship looked like. Thinking about what future visits with the soft-spoken intelligent therapist might unearth, terrified her. The only stability she'd ever found, on the job, was out of reach in the moment.

Derek had interrogated Darby. Others would tie the lose ends this time.

"How does it make you feel?" Bethany asked, sounding tired. "I try to do what's best for both of us. Am I asking too much of you?"

There was no easy answer. Bethany deserved one, that much was for sure, if not for the time she had talked Jordan out of a decision that most likely would have been fatal, then for the times she'd betrayed her. How binding was this unspoken contract? Had she really signed on for life?

Ellie had said Bethany didn't love her. That might be true. Bethany wanted things in order, no disruptions. Since everyone was so concerned about her feelings lately, Jordan should take a closer look herself.

"This isn't going to work," she said.

"You can tell after one session, really?"

"I mean us. We tried, more than once. Trying again won't change anything."

"Why, because you plan to sleep with her again?"

Jordan flinched, but Bethany wasn't done. "Did you, when you went to see her?"

Sure, that was the first thing on my mind once I got out of that hellhole. "I can't do this. I thought I could, but it's not working. I'm packing a few things tonight. I'm leaving."

"No, you're not." Bethany's sympathetic expression bordered on pity, but Jordan knew there was something else beneath. Fear. Nobody wanted to be alone. "You're still on sick leave, and you have terrible nightmares." *Who else is going to bother?* was what she didn't say.

"I know what you've done for me. I'm not taking it lightly, and I'll never forget it, but I can't be with anyone right now. Please understand."

"Come on." Bethany started the car, fastening her seatbelt in a curt angry gesture. "You're going to come back to the sessions, right? You can have your time away, it's your house after all, but you will come back."

"I don't think so."

"You don't think so. Wow."

Bethany didn't say another word until they reached their apartment and Jordan started folding clothes into a suitcase.

"You can't be by yourself. You don't even have food there."

Jordan straightened, taking in Bethany's disbelieving gaze. "I can stop by the grocery store."

"You've been planning this. So you lied to me again, what else is new?"

"I didn't lie to you. I was going to tell you, on that day. I didn't know my realtor had other plans," Jordan said coolly, making Bethany halt. She picked up the suitcase, wincing. "I apologized. More than once. Okay, the last time I was kind of pressured into it, and I wouldn't have chosen the wording, but I am sorry. Now I need you to let me go."

The panic flashing in Bethany's eyes told her she understood Jordan meant more than this moment.

"I'll be here when you come back. We both know you will."

"Goodbye, Bethany."

It was ironic that the man who had almost taken her life had helped her find a home. She had to disassociate this place from him, and when Jordan walked through the front door of her house once more, she thought she could. Fortunately, there was no urgent need for renovations. All she needed was to move in a few more boxes and clothes. Derek would help with that. She could live here comfortably, trying to gain back her balance enough so she could return to work.

She had to, now that she had a mortgage to pay on her own.

Jordan went into the bathroom, where she stripped to take a shower, for the first time in a while meeting her mirror image with defiance. *You have no idea what I survived* before *we met*, she directed at the ghost of her nightmares.

She had fooled him after all. He didn't get to decide who was in her life. Jordan wasn't the one locked up. On the contrary, she was finally free.

Chapter Nineteen

K nowing Jonathan Darby was behind bars went a long way to ease her mind. Ellie could sleep a little better at night, for which she was grateful, but there was nothing to help with her heartbreak. She knew she'd have to give Jordan the time and space she needed to come to her own conclusions. That didn't mean it wasn't hard.

Rumor had it Bethany had gone back to headquarters. Ellie had no idea if she and Jordan had continued the couples' therapy, or if they were even still trying.

Ellie had begun to resume her old life, work, hanging out with friends—working up the courage to make that call. If she didn't want to talk, Jordan could always say no. Ellie needed to know she was going to be okay. If she was honest, that wasn't all she hoped for. Until she was brave enough, she would hold on to a memory that felt increasingly unreal.

She sat next to Libby in roll call one morning, anticipating Kate and Jensen's engagement party this upcoming weekend. The sight of Derek and Jordan standing next to Sergeant Bristol jolted her quickly out of the thought.

"Phil Hobbs." Jordan pointed to the image of a grim-looking man, in late forties or early fifties maybe, that was projected on the wall. He escaped from a county prison last night, still has lots of contacts in the area. He's in for aggravated assault and second-degree murder but likes to get his hands dirty on everything illegal, guns, drugs, gambling. Any hints, you report straight to us, and don't approach him without backup. This man is extremely dangerous. He injured two guards, one of them critically."

"If he feels cornered, he will shoot first," Henderson added. "Be careful."

While this was reason for concern, for everyone in the room, Ellie could feel her attention drift, her gaze drawn to Jordan. She looked ready to be back in the arena, in charge. Ellie was happy and relieved to see her like that again, though she hadn't forgotten other memories they shared, of a darker, terrifying world. They wouldn't let the monsters that walked in that world win.

"Officer Harding."

"I'll wait in the car," Libby said with a knowing smile. "Don't take too long."

Ellie turned around to face the woman who had occupied her fantasies and worries in the past weeks. Her heart was pounding. These feelings were impossible to turn off.

"How are you doing?" Jordan asked, her voice soft and warm like Ellie remembered it from other circumstances.

"Good. I'm good, but I think I should be asking you that question."

Jordan gave her a wry smile. "Better? I think that sums it up. It's good to be back, even on a day I have to find out a lowlife like Hobbs is back on the streets."

"We'll find him," Ellie said without hesitation.

"Yes, we will. Be careful out there."

Jordan touched her shoulder for a brief moment, a gesture of encouragement, but it felt as if had they been alone, she would have held her back, pulled her close. Maybe that was Ellie's imagination, but it felt good anyway.

"Always."

She hesitated, waiting for any sign, anything hinting at a chance that they could ever go back to what they'd had for a brief time.

"By the way...I'm getting the rest of my things in this weekend," Jordan said, nothing more, but between the lines, Ellie could read enough to nurture the hope she'd been clinging to for the past weeks.

"You kept the house?"

"Yeah."

"That's good."

"Ellie, are you coming?" Libby called from behind the wheel of the squad car.

"Looks like you've got to go," Jordan said with a smile. "I'll see you soon."

"You will."

Ellie walked away, certain she hadn't yet collected everything life had to offer to her, reveling in a gesture that felt warm and bittersweet and too fleeting.

Time would tell.

Acknowledgments

Thank you —

Dominique – for everything.

May Dawney, for the stunning cover art that made all the difference for Jordan and Ellie's (ongoing) story.

All my readers who have embarked on the journey with these characters.

This is the series I wanted to exist for a long time, and because of you, now, it does.

About the Author

B arbara Winkes writes sapphic crime drama and Christ-
mas romance. She loves writing characters who get the
job done, whether it's stopping a predator or saving cherished
traditions—while still making time for love. She lives with her
wife in Quebec City.

barbarawinkes.com

Also by Barbara Winkes

The Crossing Lines Trilogy
Undercover
Redemption
Vengeance

The Connected Series
Promised to the Queen
Drawn to the Enemy
Tempted by the Protector